CHAPTER 1

Two spiritual beings met in the command center of a spacecraft orbiting Earth. The first was a tall, slender gentleman whose regal bearing was accentuated by his formal black military uniform trimmed in gold. His piercing, gunmetal-gray eyes burned with unwavering intensity, strikingly contrasting with his albino complexion and giving him an otherworldly presence.

Also adorned in impeccable formal attire, Caligastia radiated confidence that verged on arrogance. His voice filled the space as he declared, "I am being considered for the post of Planetary Prince of Earth, a position for which I am eminently well qualified. This is my sixth endorsement from the Celestial Fathers, a testament to my persistence and capabilities."

A heavy silence descended in response to his proclamation. The black-clad gentleman, the System Sovereign of Radania, leaned back in his chair and glanced upward, eyes half closed, as if in mental contact with unseen observers. The hint of a curt smile appeared on his face.

Caligastia, an imposing figure standing seven feet tall with a muscular, sculpted physique and a bronzed visage that spoke of might, slowly strode toward a transparent crystalline window. Gazing past the darkness of space, he marveled at the beauty of a continent blanketed by Earth's fifth glacial advance. *At last, a planet I can call my own,* he thought.

The System Sovereign slowly straightened in his chair. With a dismissive gesture, he apparently concluded other worldly matters.

Caligastia ran his fingers through his short blonde hair, briefly admiring his reflection in the window. He turned and took a step towards his superior. "As you are fully aware," he said brashly, with pose, "I have accumulated an enviable record of loyalty and devotion to the welfare of the universe of my origin."

The Sovereign took a sip of water directly from a pitcher resting on the glass table. After a few moments of uncomfortable silence, Caligastia continued. "No one has richer preparatory experience or brighter prospects for success than I."

No response. *Why am I being ignored?* Caligastia thought, his anger quickly rising.

With a scornful shake of his head, the Sovereign finally acknowledged Caligastia, directing a look of disdain at him. "Your petition for the post of planetary prince has been disapproved on numerous previous occasions," he said, his voice resonating with quiet authority, "yet you persist in your ambition."

Taken aback by the cold reception, Caligastia bowed his head slightly, his pride momentarily faltering. "The delay in my receiving a position such as this is due to circumstances beyond my control, sir. I am fully capable of handling every task required of a planetary prince."

"Are you saying the Celestial Fathers do not have the ability to decide when prospects are ready for advancement?" the Sovereign said with a sneer, his eyes narrowing. "Or are you saying Gabriel just doesn't understand you?"

Caligastia, his face hardening, strolled to the other side of the room. *Why am I being treated with disrespect?*

The Sovereign made his way to the monitor on his desk. With a smooth flick of his wrist, the screen came alive with a flurry of flashing data. Turning back toward Caligastia, his form subtly expanded, his presence radiating intimidating authority. "I have inspected the credentials of ninety-nine of your staff and one is missing."

"I have yet to decide upon my third in command," Caligastia stated without a hint of trepidation.

A wry chuckle escaped the Sovereign as his physique gradually returned to its customary form. "Why are you having difficulty, Caligastia? Tens of millions possess the proper ascension training and the leadership qualities necessary to serve as your third in command."

Caligastia's expression hardened, "That is precisely the problem, sir. I desire someone who is lacking in ascension training."

Eyebrows were raised.

Caligastia, sensing that he'd hit upon a sensitive subject, escalated his argument. "I feel far too much time and energy are expended on training ascending mortals." *As do you.*

"As do I," said the Sovereign, intrigued. A moment of contemplation transpired. "Continue. Who will head your staff on Earth?"

Caligastia, beads of sweat forming at his temples, strolled to the refreshment table. *Now I'm in control,* he thought, pouring himself a drink. "My second in command will be Hammone of the Lanonandek order. My chief of staff and third in command will come from an early ascension training school."

Again, Caligastia walked to the crystalline wall, drink in hand, and looked down at Earth. He stood with his back to the Sovereign. "I believe that a personality with a lack of credentials will be easy to control and manipulate if support of the staff is needed in the future."

In an instant, the Sovereign's demeanor shifted to one of unbridled fury. "Just what, Caligastia, do you anticipate happening that will require the manipulation of your staff?" His entire body visibly expanded with a forceful, inner rage. "Your staff will unwaveringly support you and follow your lead without the need for any such manipulation!"

At that precise moment, a deafening boom echoed as a dazzling flash of energy erupted just outside the craft. Caligastia's glass shattered on the floor.

"Should you harbor any doubts about the unwavering loyalty of any member of your staff," the Sovereign commanded, "remove them immediately! Is that understood?"

Caligastia spun around. "Yes, sir," he said. *Priority number one, staff loyalty,* he thought, his mind reeling.

The Sovereign then fixed him with a final, imperious gaze. "Do you have anything further to add before these proceedings are formally enacted?"

"No, my lord," Caligastia replied, blood drained from his face.

The spiritual being's tone was deep and ominous. "I, Lucifer, System Sovereign of Radania, absolute ruler of 608 inhabited worlds located in over five hundred different physical solar systems, now officially proclaim you, Caligastia, Planetary Prince of Earth." Lucifer vanished.

Chapter 2

The classroom's front wall was transformed into a vast cosmic canvas, an immense screen alive with swirling crab nebulae, luminous colored gases and millions of flickering stars. The display vibrated and radiated an intense, spiritual glow that seemed to breathe the essence of life into these young, eager minds.

"A part of our local universe, Nebadon," whispered the schoolteacher. The modest, unadorned interior of the small classroom boasted rugged planked hardwood floors, freshly whitewashed walls, towering double-hung windows and a lofty nine-foot ceiling. She paused for a moment, allowing her gaze to wander over her class. A gentle smile warmed her face as she caught sight of Lisa and Mendal sitting in the front row, their youthful expressions brimming with anticipation and wonder.

Mendal exuded a serious contemplative air. His short- cropped brown hair and baby blue eyes had the innocent look of a country boy untouched by the city. Beside him, Lisa, with her impeccably braided ash blond hair cascading down her back, offered a playful, coquettish smile as she tenderly squeezed Mendal's hand.

He knowingly returned her glance. Together they took a bodiless journey out of one of the open windows of this one room schoolhouse and danced amongst the chirping of birds and chattering of squirrels.

The teacher cleared her throat. Mendal quickly straightened in his chair, his face pink with embarrassment. Although he knew better, he just couldn't resist Lisa's overtures. She gave the teacher an it-was-his-idea look, then postured prim and proper. The students giggled.

The teacher resumed her lecture when she was confident she had the children's full attention. As she addressed them, the group of fifty students, half boys and half girls, studied the screen and their teacher with enthusiasm. Each wore unique, casual apparel. They needed neither notebooks nor pencils; they were able to absorb information instantaneously, though each at his or her own level.

As the teacher recited the morning lesson, she strolled around the room, laying her hand on the shoulder of each student. "All planets that are inhabited by evolutionary mortal creatures have assigned to them a planetary ruler. These Planetary Princes are in immediate command to the System Sovereigns."

An image of a distant galaxy in the Ursa Major constellation unfurled on the screen. "Behold, the Pinwheel Galaxy Messier," the teacher declared, extending her arm with gracefully. Taking a few measured moments to collect her thoughts, the teacher seated herself on the edge of her desk. Suddenly, her head jerked upward by a sudden force, a mental broadcast that crackled through her consciousness.

"I've just been informed that this will be Mendal's last class," she announced softly, glancing meaningfully at him. The pause that followed was heavy with expectancy before she reiterated the message. "Mendal will now undergo his final testing. If he passes, he will immediately embark upon his ascension career."

The room erupted into a flurry of chatter and excited gossip. Lisa's startled gasp punctuated the commotion, for she and none of the other students had anticipated Mendal might be ready to graduate this quickly.

Again, the teacher's head snapped upward, triggered by another mental transmission. With an assured nod, she quieted the room. "Lisa will accompany Mendal and Radania will serve as the launch point for their ascension," she explained. "They will commence at the very bottom of the evolutionary cycle, specifically with the human level of development."

A stunned Tyler couldn't help but interject, his voice filled with incredulity: "You mean Mendal is ready to begin his ascension career? And at the human level? Isn't that regarded as the most challenging in all physical reality?"

The teacher hesitated, uncertainty flickering across her features, as she tilted her head upward. After a moment of reflective silence, she slowly offered a tentative nod, confirming the reality of the situation.

In a heartbeat, the children swarmed around Lisa and Mendal. One close friend of Lisa leaned in and whispered, "Everyone has always assumed you'd be the one ready for graduation, but how could Mendal possibly be?"

Another friend placed a comforting hand on her shoulder, softly asking, "Will you become a Life Carrier, Lisa?"

Lisa's voice wavered as she stammered, "I hope so," revealing her uncertainty about the abrupt twist her life had just taken.

Not to be outdone by his companion, Mendal added, "I want to be a Life Carrier, too." The two then rose from their seats and embraced each other warmly, a silent pact of mutual support in the face of destiny.

Tyler, unable to resist a final jab, teased playfully, "Yeah, we all know you just want to follow your girlfriend. What Lisa wants, Mendal wants." This prompted several of the other students to nod in earnest agreement.

With the session drawing to a close, the teacher shut off the wall screen and quietly exited the room.

As the discussion lingered, one classmate's voice broke through the crowd with genuine concern, "We don't have to live actual physical lives to advance. Do you realize what you're getting into?"

Mendal, however, flashed a fearless smile as he strode confidently out of the classroom. "If I'm going to take a ride through life, I want it to be the wildest ride possible." he declared.

CHAPTER 3

A group of six scientists and a colleague entered the doorway leading to their early morning destination: the Life Implantation Laboratory on the planet Jerusem, the capital of the Radania galaxy. The six scientists were not human, although their form was human-like. The colleague had a hazy, ghost-like facade and a haughty demeanor that commanded respect.

"The life patterns for Earth are complete," announced one of the scientists to the ghost-like creature. "This was a time-consuming project but an unequivocal success in every condition you and the System Sovereign stipulated."

"So, you're saying the mistake that happened on Venesaro will not be repeated?" said the ghost-like creature with a hint of indignation. "Am I hearing you correctly?"

"Yes, sir. We have gone over computer simulations more than 100,000 times and each time the results are identical. This experiment in creating a life form new to our universe of Nebadon will be successful."

Another figure suddenly appeared. The scientists stepped back in surprise at this unexpected visit from the System Sovereign of Radania. Everyone bowed in respect and remained in that position until Lucifer spoke. "I want a full verbal report," he said calmly.

One of the humanoid scientists stepped forward and proceeded with the report. "With the cooperation and support of spiritual forces and supernatural powers, we have finished the long and tedious task of originating the life patterns for Earth, an evolving planet in the Radania galaxy," he said.

"It is now the job of the Life Carriers to transplant these newly created life patterns in three designated water sites on Earth: the Eurasian-African, the Australasian and the Greenland-Americas. The sites were carefully chosen to ensure that each great land mass will carry this life with it in its warm water seas, as the land subsequently separates." The scientist bowed his head and stepped back in line with his colleagues.

Lucifer removed some papers from the briefcase he held and quickly read through them. "Why was the experiment in the creation of a new life form and its implantation a total failure on Venesaro?" he asked, irritated.

No one dared answer. "I must be assured that a disaster of that magnitude will not be repeated," Lucifer snapped. "As you are fully aware, failure in this mission warrants revocation of the material status of all involved."

"We have planted a mutation in the evolutionary process that will guarantee success," another of the scientist said, his voice monotone, his body robotic. "Instead of straight linear revolution, from era to era radically new species of animal life will appear and will not evolve gradually in small variations. They will appear as full-fledged new orders of life and they will appear suddenly.

"All living organisms on Earth," the scientist added, "will attain spiritual unity and survive or they will fall short of this goal and cease to exist. The same will eventually happen to man himself. If he is unable to attain cosmic harmony, he will cease to exist as a race, as happened on Venesaro."

"We won't let that happen on Earth, will we?" the ghost-like creature said emphatically. "I value my existence as I'm sure you do as well."

The scientists, in legitimate fear, shook their heads and muttered in unison, "No, sir, we won't."

After a few moments of apparent mental interaction with Lucifer, the ghost-like creature continued. "A new spiritual entity will appear on Earth, in time, to help with human development. This being, who will function halfway between the angelic realms and human reality, will make a great difference in man's fight to survive, as will increased use of angels."

"No mistakes, miscalculations or accidents will be tolerated," said Lucifer, his eyes narrowing. With a brisk nod to the ghost-like creature, Lucifer vanished.

The scientists returned to working on their respective projects. After a few minutes of discomforting silence, one scientist turned to another standing next to him. "Lucifer is still here in spirit," he said, glancing around surreptitiously. "I can definitely feel his presence."

"He's always here," his colleague nodded. "We just can't see him. He watches our every move."

CHAPTER 4

Stepping into the principal's office, Mendal settled into the solitary chair available, a faint creak breaking the silence as he did so. The air was thick with anticipation.

The principal, reading messages from the monitor on his desk, seemed oblivious to his presence. His appearance was as Mendal imagined it would be: a slightly overweight physique dressed in a simple, dark gray jacket and white shirt, thinning blue-gray hair and a meaty face. His fatherly facade was comforting.

"Mendal, the results from your finals are in and you have passed," the principal announced with a warm smile that crinkled the corners of his eyes. Rising from his imposing mahogany desk, the principal gestured for Mendal to join him by the expansive wall screen. "We are proud of your accomplishments here at The Academy."

The monitor displayed a message, which he solemnly read aloud. "Life does not spontaneously appear in the universes; the Life Carriers must initiate it on the barren planets. After planting this life on such new worlds, they remain there for long periods to nurture, support and develop this fragile existence."

Mendal knew they were taking a risk considering him for this important position and sometimes he wondered, *Why are they taking such a risk?* "Yes, sir, this is all very clear," Mendal said, "and I realize no other Life Carrier is as inexperienced as I, but this will in no way affect my performance."

The image on the monitor shifted, revealing the young planet Earth, its surface partially veiled by masses of clouds. The principal shook Mendal's hand. "As this sphere is relatively insignificant, it would be an honorable start for a young, inexperienced personality such as yourself. I see no reason not to let you participate in the implantation of life on Earth. This will be a truly unique learning experience for you, Mendal, in a safe, out of the way part of the universe. You are now worthy to become a Life Carrier and the sphere Earth will be your destination."

A surge of exhilaration coursed through Mendal and he whooped, his exuberant voice reverberating down the hallways. The principal's expression shifted into a frown, a silent admonishment for the outburst. Mendal, overtaken by a brief wave of embarrassment, quickly regained his composure, nodded respectfully and exited the office.

CHAPTER 5

Mendal and his two associates arrived at their designated meeting point on Earth, nestled within the vast Eurasian-African life implantation region. Before them unfolded a breathtaking panorama: a lush forest draped in vibrant greenery, interspersed with cascading waterfalls under the warm caress of the summer sun. Their campsite lay gently against a stream whose waters wound their way toward a distant, shimmering ocean bay.

At the edge of the campsite, the tall, ivory-skinned female Life Carrier took a moment to unwind as she readied herself for the new day. She stretched her long limbs, feeling the tautness in her muscles, then moved with an effortless, measured grace toward the stream nearby, an intricately designed instrument pack slung over her shoulder.

Upon reaching the water's edge, Lisa knelt and submerged the instrument into the shimmering water, testing it for traces of sodium chloride. Each of her actions was precise, her fingers moving with a practiced ease.

After finishing her morning work, Lisa ascended the steep, earthen embankment. She made her way toward the expansive research facility that was fully equipped with an array of high-tech equipment, each piece meticulously designed to support their scientific endeavors.

There, standing quietly with a demeanor carved from experience, Senior Life Carrier Don awaited her arrival. His jet-black hair and sharply chiseled Asian features lent him an air of quiet authority as he greeted her. "Lisa, how's the testing going today? Any increase in the sodium chloride content?" he asked.

"Miniscule," Lisa replied softly. "However, every little increase draws us nearer to our goal." A subtle smile brightened her face before a wistful sigh escaped her lips. "To be completely honest, Don, I wish I could work here forever. This serene, earthbound existence is utterly addictive. I could live on Earth forever."

Don's lips curled in a light, knowing chuckle as he reminded her, "Remember, we only have half a million years to go."

Lisa rolled her eyes as they entered the building. Lisa spotted Mendal, hunched over a computer terminal tucked away in a dim corner, completely absorbed in his work with the single-minded focus of a man who lived solely for his project.

Mendal's tall, lanky figure towered over his companions, yet he seemed almost fragile. His hair clung untidily to his head and his rounded shoulders betrayed the long hours spent slouched over technology. His slender face remained unshaven, a rugged testament to his dedication.

Breaking the silence, Lisa remarked with an involuntary smile, "I'm glad you appointed him as our computer expert instead of me."

"So am I, Lisa," Don replied warmly, a teasing edge in his voice. "Computers might never be your forte, but I promise you, one of these days you'll get some advanced training."

Rising, Mendal stretched his arms as if discarding the weight of the world and moved toward his colleagues. But before he could reach them, all three abruptly jerked their heads upward as an urgent, shrieking computer warning echoed through the room.

In perfect synchrony, Lisa and Mendal raced to the nearest terminals, their hearts quickening as they deciphered the rapidly cascading data on their screens. "Code BR433, Don," Lisa announced calmly, her voice steady even as her eyes flicked to Mendal, seeking confirmation.

"Yes, confirmed," Mendal replied without hesitation. "This is a level one emergency, Don. Can you specify the parameters?"

From behind his terminal, Don's tone grew grave as he interpreted the incoming data. "A series of corrupted drives have disrupted the computer-controlled life-purification system."

Lisa's fingers hovered over her keyboard, poised for a command. "You'll have to restore their memory, Don. Just how serious is this contamination?"

Don's eyes widened in alarm as he quickly calculated the threat. "There isn't enough time to manually repair each drive. This might even result in the complete corruption of Earth's entire biological life pattern supply!"

In a fit of urgency, Mendal sprang up and dashed to a storage compartment to retrieve a sleek mental-linkage device. "I'm going to network directly with the computer," he declared. "We've invested far too much time and effort to lose everything now."

Lisa hurried to Mendal's side, her eyes pleading for guidance, while Don continued frantically calculating the risk. "Contamination will commence within ten minutes," he warned, the gravity of his words sinking in with each passing moment.

"Lisa, hook me up to the computer terminal immediately!" Mendal shouted. With practiced efficiency, she connected a slender wire from Mendal's left temple to the waiting terminal. A sudden surge of electrical current seized his neck muscles, causing his eyes to roll back briefly as he spoke through clenched teeth, "Don't disconnect me, Lisa. I'm searching the files."

Several heart-pounding minutes passed. Finally, Don broke the tense silence: "Nothing's changed. We've got only three minutes left, Mendal."

Undeterred by the faltering psychic-aided method, Mendal bolted to the door of an adjoining chamber. "I'm going to spirit-activate the link," he announced with resolve, "and halt the contamination."

"No, Mendal!" Don cried out franticly. "That will cost you your mortal life. Lisa, stop him immediately!"

Lisa's gaze was locked on Mendal, her eyes wide with both admiration and sorrow, yet she remained silent and did nothing to deter him.

"Remember, I'm in command here, Mendal," Don insisted, his voice rising as he dashed from his desk. "There must be another solution." Grabbing Mendal's arm in a desperate bid for control, he tried to pull him back from the brink.

In that fleeting moment, a storm of conflicting impulses swirled within Mendal. He hesitated just for a second. *I can't let this disaster happen*, he thought resolutely. *Earth won't get a second chance.*

With a determined pull, he jerked free from Don's grasp, opened the chamber door and disappeared inside. Within moments, a brilliant flash of blue energy enveloped him as his spirit merged with the computer. His physical form crumbled to the floor, utterly lifeless.

Don and Lisa rushed into the chamber. Without wasting another second, Don smashed open their emergency RRK with the decisive swing of his hand and retrieved a myocardial jet injector.

He moved to Mendal's inert body and quickly tore open his shirt to expose his chest. Methodically, he positioned the instrument exactly over Mendal's heart and adjusted the setting with a sense of urgent precision. Taking a deep, steadying breath, he pushed the injection button and bellowed, "Live, Mendal!"

Yet, after ten agonizing minutes of desperate resuscitation efforts, both Don and Lisa were forced to concede defeat. Mendal was gone. In a hushed, reverent tone, Lisa whispered upward as if addressing an unseen observer. "Mendal's unwavering loyalty to us and to our experiment in life-pattern initiation will ensure that our mission endures. He was truly a devoted Life Carrier."

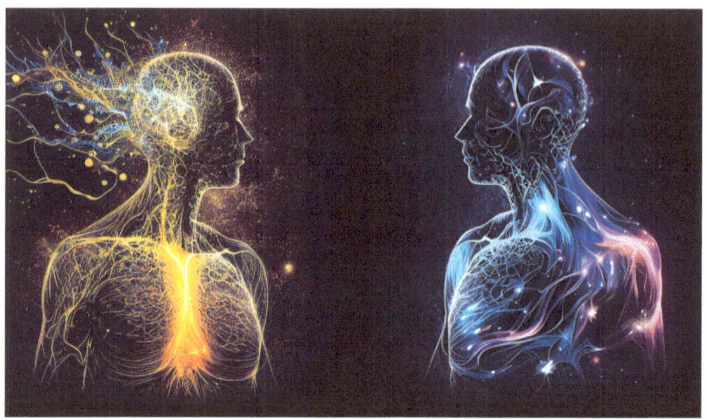

***

In the dim, otherworldly light of a distant command center within his home planet, Lucifer allowed himself a knowing smile as he watched the entire harrowing episode unfold on one of fifty pulsating monitors. "He's the one, isn't he?" sneered Satan.

"Yes," Lucifer replied, "Yes, he is."

CHAPTER 6

"Where am I?" Mendal muttered, his voice barely audible as he stepped instinctively through the doorway into an office that resonated with a disquieting sense of familiarity. His eyes darted around the room as his pulse quickened; every detail recalled memories of a place he'd visited before.

This was the very room where he had received his Life Carrier assignment and the pieces of his memory quickly fell back into place. A nagging question pierced his thoughts: *Did I stop the contamination?*

The principal emerged from an entryway behind his desk, his presence carried both authority and warmth. "Yes, you did," he asserted softly. "But your existence as a Life Carrier on Earth is now complete. You have returned to the Academy."

Mendal, his body now reflecting the maturity of thirty years, was visibly overwhelmed by confusion and disorientation. Every fiber of his being seemed to wrestle with the revelation, as if time itself shifted under his feet.

"Mendal, it is good to have you back," the principal said cheerfully. "It is rare indeed for a student to return for reassignment." The sincerity in his voice mingled with a hint of excitement, a promise that something extraordinary was about to unfold.

With an encouraging smile, the principal drew his arm around Mendal's shoulders. "Normally, only one life is permitted on Earth," he explained while leading him down a narrow corridor into an adjacent room. "However, because of your steadfast loyalty to your mission, the Most Highs have conveyed that you may be granted another." His words rang as if the cosmic balance had shifted in Mendal's favor.

The room into which they stepped was arranged with a cushion sofa and three tables with chairs. "It appears that someone of significant importance has taken a keen interest in you and there's even a visitor awaiting," the principal remarked before departing.

Left alone, Mendal stood amid the room's quiet austerity. He remembered his previous experience in the research facility and had full retention of his knowledge as a Life Carrier.

A new thought flickered in his mind; *perhaps a quantum probability computer is hidden somewhere within these walls.* Driven by equal parts curiosity and duty, he began to scrutinize the room, his eyes searching every surface for concealed technology.

His attention was captivated by large paintings on the wall behind the sofa, which seemed to beckon with an air of mystery. One of the paintings was a little worn on the edges and, with a deliberate tug, the panel swung downward to reveal its hidden secret.

Behind it lay a built-in compartment, housing a quantum probability computer. The computer's complex circuitry and intricate components hinted at untold computational power and potential.

I guess it won't hurt to take a quick look, Mendal reasoned internally, despite apprehension welling in his chest. *I want to see where Earth's headed.*

A hesitation crept over him as he considered the strict boundaries of his authority. *It's against the rules,* he thought, stepping back toward his chair. Suddenly an overwhelming command echoed in his mind: *Do it, Mendal!* He froze. An intense, invisible force suddenly filled the room. It was as if the very air itself was alive and pulsated with formidable energy.

Do it now! The silent command sent a shiver down his spine. His heart pounding against his ribcage, Mendal turned back to face the computer. His intense stare into the heart of the devise brought it to life. "Iris recognition software has been activated. Identity has been confirmed," declared a disembodied voice. "Top level access to Earth probabilities has been granted."

That was easy, he thought, with a tinge of guilt. *Maybe too easy?* As he studied the screen, his eyes widened and his body tensed. In a desperate bid to understand, he hit the replay button, only to be met with the same startling revelation. *This can't be true,* he thought, petrified by the emerging reality.

The sudden sound of footsteps broke his concentration. Mendal quickly returned the computer to its hidden position. He turned to see Lisa entering the room, "Lisa!" he exclaimed, drawing in a deep, steadying breath before striding towards her.

Her smile and embrace were warm and enveloping. "I didn't think I would ever see you again," she whispered as she held him tightly for a few moments. "I disturbed you. What were you working on?"

"It's nothing," Mendal quickly replied.

"I've heard you'll be given another physical life on Earth," Lisa said softly.

"Nothing's official yet," said Mendal, "but it's in the works." Soon, he hoped. He was anxious to get back to work.

"Do you know what your assignment will be?" she asked. "I'd be honored to have you return to work with Don and I."

"They haven't said yet," Mendal replied, "but since my life will be on Earth, I imagine I'll be back with you two."

Lisa smiled. "Don and I put in a reinstatement request. That should help your cause."

"Thanks, Lisa." Mendal put his arm around her and gently squeezed. He couldn't help but think of all the good times they had as kids back in school and as Life Carriers. It seemed to him as though they'd always been together. "How's Don?" he asked.

"Don's great, as usual. You can't break that spirit of his," Lisa said with a gentle smile. "He had to stay. If he takes his eyes off Earth for a moment, he thinks he'll miss something important."

"Yes, that's Don for sure," Mendal said with a smile.

"Our time-relation just changed," Lisa added, a touch of excitement in her voice. "We've slowed down the time-enhancement quantum computer to 100 years per day and can control it to present time, if needed. We had been running it up to 10,000 years per day."

Without warning, the principal re-entered the room, his expression serious. "Lisa, Don needs you back on Earth," he stated, his voice tight with urgency.

Lisa, clearly annoyed by the interruption, rolled her eyes and glanced briefly at the principal. With a tender gesture, she pressed a light kiss to Mendal's forehead and whispered, "It's been wonderful seeing you, Mendal. I'm so glad I came, though I wish we had more time."

Mendal stood and pressed a passionate kiss to Lisa's lips, his gaze smoldering with longing and resolve. "Goodbye, Lisa," he whispered, his eyes reflecting the intensity of emotions he couldn't quite conceal. Lisa left the room.

The principal walked Mendal into an adjoining room. "Time is crucial," the principal stressed. "I had no idea you would receive this appointment. For now, you need to catch up on the history of man. A lot of Earth time has passed, and you need a quick overview as to what has happened."

Mendal, awestruck at the sight of the massive simulation computer on the wall, walked to a small circular table. The moment he sat in the chair, the wall computer turned on and began displaying information about the history of man on Earth.

"Early one morning after nearly nine hundred generations since the origin of the dawn mammals, a Primate couple gave birth to two exceptional creatures, the first two true human beings, Andon and Fonta, the actual ancestors of mankind.

"Earth was registered as an inhabited world when the first two human beings, the twins, were eleven years old, and before they had become the parents of the first-born of the second generation of actual human beings. And the archangel message from Salvington, on this occasion of formal planetary recognition, closed with these words:

"Man-mind has appeared on 606 of Radania, and these parents of the new race shall be called Andon and Fonta. And all archangels pray that these creatures may speedily be endowed with the personal indwelling of the gift of the spirit of the Universal Father.

"Cultures and civilizations continued to rise and fall over the next half-million years, with the extinction of the human race at one time a distinct possibility. Civilizations of great promise such as the Heidelberg race, the Foxhall peoples, the Badonan tribes and the Neanderthal races rose and then deteriorated and, ultimately, annihilated themselves due to superior beings procreating with the inferior and the incessant nature of man to fight with people he considered different from himself.

"Civilizations in the northern latitudes tended to flourish while those in the southern regions of Earth stagnated. Man always progressed only in the open and higher altitudes, due to cold and hunger stimulating activity, invention and creativity.

"The Badonan tribes of the northwestern highlands of India engaged themselves in great struggle and, for over one hundred years, this war raged. When the fight was finally finished, only one hundred families remained, but they were the most intelligent and desirable of the still living descendants of Andon and Fonta.

"These Andonites were fearless hunters who lived exclusively on flesh, with the exception of a few berries and fruits. They preferred living under the shelter of overhanging cliffs along the rivers and, when possible, near the edges of forests. They fashioned many tools using flint, bone and wood, including stone axes and harpoons. These people gained a high level of intelligence which some of their regressing descendants, those traveling east and south and subsequently mixing with animal cousins, were unable to obtain.

"Among the highland Badonites, a startling new event occurred. For the first time in the entire Radania system, a couple, the Sangik family, began suddenly producing exceptionally intelligent children whose skin manifested a distinct color when exposed to sunlight. The color became more pronounced the older the child grew, and when they eventually mated and produced offspring, the resultant child had the color of the Sangik parent.

"Of the nineteen children born to the Sangik parents, five were red, two were orange, four were yellow, two green, and two were indigo. This was unusual because, on every other evolutionary planet in Radania, the red people appeared first. For ages they evolved and then, one by one, the other colors made their appearance. The simultaneous appearance of all six races on Earth, and in one family, had never happened before.

"The emergence of the earlier Andonites was also a rare event, for never before in Radania has a race evolved and roamed the world before the appearance of the evolutionary races of color. The experiment in modifying the quality of life in Radania had resulted in an unique history for the planet Earth, a unique and unusual history that gained the attention not only of Lucifer, the System Sovereign of Radania, but his Creator Son, Michael of Nebadon, as well."

Mendel, finished with the brief historical update, entered the principal's office to receive his new assignment.

CHAPTER 7

Concurrent with the appearance of the six colored or Sangik races, the Planetary Prince of Earth, arrived on the planet. There were almost one-half billion primitive human beings on Earth at the time of the prince's arrival and they were well scattered over Europe, Asia and Africa. The prince's headquarters, established in Mesopotamia, was at about the center of world population.

Daligastia, proud son of Caligastia and mayor of the towering city of Dalamatia, relished his morning walks. The crisp silence of the early hours was punctuated only by the delicate chorus of birdsong echoing through the trees. Every day, without fail, he took this chance to stroll beyond the imposing forty-foot walls that encircled his beloved city.

Years spent surviving on a raw, unrefined planet had not only toughened him but had also lent impressive muscularity to his initially genetically sculpted form. His sun-kissed blond hair shimmered against his striking Nordic features, a look that, combined with his natural charisma, reinforced his firm hold over Dalamatia.

Much like his father, he inherited not only a fierce, legendary temper but also, intriguingly, the near-mystical ability to influence those around him with only a few measured words.

In the distance, the mingled scents of smoke and the crackle of campfires signaled the start of yet another day among the local tribespeople. Daligastia smiled at the unhurried, harmonious pace of Earth life as he began the short journey back to the vibrant city. Earth's very first capital was a beacon of civilization nestled in a landscape where nature and humanity intermingled.

As he ambled along the meadow, a swirling cloud of dust suddenly caught his attention. A solitary figure sprinted down the northern hillside, waving frantically against the golden light of morning as he neared. Daligastia moved quickly toward the center of the field, pausing to await the arrival of his aide.

"Sir, a seraphic transport has just descended from Lucifer's home planet," the young aide panted, his words tumbling out in a breathless stammer.

Daligastia's eyes widened in surprise as he processed the unexpected news. "What? Lucifer isn't scheduled for arrival for another six months." He hesitated for a few moments, then called out to the aid. "Return to the city immediately. Inform my father of Lucifer's unexpected arrival. He'll know the proper course of action."

"Yes, sir," came the reply as the aide turned toward the city, only to be interrupted by the sudden appearance of the System Sovereign's transport. Glowing silver under the bright morning sun, the craft rose gracefully from a hillside landing site to the north. Hovering momentarily, it positioned itself directly above the two men. Out of radiant light, five imposing figures materialized within mere feet of Daligastia, while the aide dashed back toward the ancient city walls.

Lucifer emerged first, a presence shrouded in austere dignity. Clad in a loose-fitting, full-length black military uniform, he wore an inscrutable expression upon his ghostly white face. His straight, shoulder-length hair, as dark as spilled ink, framed a visage that held no trace of emotion. Towering at six feet nine inches, he possessed an almost skeletal silhouette, as if the fabric of his coat barely concealed the essence of his being.

One of Lucifer's four lieutenants broke the tense silence. "Lucifer will not speak during this meeting," he declared in a firm, resonant tone. All four men shared uncanny similarities: each stood an imposing six feet six inches tall with square-jaws and meticulously cut short, buckskin-colored hair. Their black and gold military uniforms glistened subtly in the early light. "I will handle everything. My name is Karl."

Daligastia replied with a brisk nod but couldn't help but mentally note the striking uniformity and polished presence of these "pretty boys." Attempting to regain control of the situation, Daligastia announced, with measured pride, "The headquarters of our great planet is known as Dalamatia, my lord. This region boasts an exemplary climate and landscape, with unparalleled access to both the mighty ocean and a verdant forest that shelters native Earth tribes. In time, every inhabitant of Earth will find passage to Dalamatia by land, sea and air."

Lucifer then drifted a few paces back toward the green meadow. Standing statuesque, he slowly tilted his head upward. With a series of long, deep breaths, he appeared to slip into a meditative state, an image at once both captivating and mystifying.

Daligastia, bewildered by Lucifer's odd behavior, grabbed Karl's arm. "What is Lucifer doing?" Karl jerked away from the grasp and looked to the others. The four exchanged nervous glances, but no one spoke.

"I said, what is he doing?" Daligastia snapped, his face hardening. *Lucifer's lieutenants or not, I refuse to tolerate insubordination.*

"Quiet, you'll disturb him," Karl hissed, glaring at Daligastia defiantly.

"You've got one minute to explain yourself," Daligastia said in a cool, icy whisper, *before I put you in your place.*

Karl took a few calculated steps toward Lucifer, his eyes focused on Lucifer's slouched, stationary torso, then conferred with his colleagues. All three nodded in agreement moments later. Karl motioned Daligastia aside. "Lucifer has sent a portion of himself to a conference today, sir," Karl said, his voice bold and full of respect. "It is one in a series of consultations with select Planetary Princes of Radania."

"Is that why he looks so drained, so devoid of life?" Daligastia pressed, his gaze fixed intently on Lucifer. Taking a step closer, he unexpectedly found his path obstructed by the four looming figures.

"Do not disturb him or ask any questions, sir," Karl implored. "The situation in Radania is reaching a critical juncture. Lucifer must now persuade the princes—." His words faltered under the weight of the looks from his comrades.

"Persuade the princes of what, lieutenant?" Daligastia snapped, his voice sharpening with barely contained indignation. "And why were neither my father nor I informed of these consultations?"

Karl's response was ice-cold and unyielding. "He will inform Caligastia at the appropriate time."

Frustrated by Karl's dismissive tone in the face of his pointed question, Daligastia lunged forward, his eyes burning as his fists clenched with the surge of hot blood. Yet before he could make contact, a calming hand from Lucifer landed upon his shoulder, diffusing the sudden eruption of tensions.

Caligastia materialized from a suddenly visible seraphic transport, his presence authoritative and composed. The transport vanished. Caligastia signaled for his son to return to the city and gently but firmly escorted Lucifer aside for a private exchange.

"Beyond the boundaries of Dalamatia reside the primitive human tribes, groups as diverse as they are numerous," Caligastia stated, sweeping his arm grandly toward the dense forest. "The inaugural students of our esteemed schools will be one hundred carefully chosen survivors from the very first humans of Earth. These individuals represent the finest strands of that singular race. The surgeons of Gallon will bestow upon them the life circuit implants, marking the beginning of a transformation."

Lucifer's expression, while still inscrutable, seemed to brighten at the news. Caligastia continued passionately, "During this procedure, vital samples of their life plasm will be extracted. These enhanced beings will serve my staff and be trained to become educators and leaders for their people."

Glancing briefly at Karl, Lucifer interjected with calm authority, "Have the constructed bodies for your staff been completed?"

"Indeed, they have," Caligastia replied, a note of satisfaction in his voice. "Those bodies reside safely in the Planetary Health and Life Center. According to the Senior Life Carrier, the process was flawlessly executed."

"Very good," Lucifer managed with a nod. "Please continue, Caligastia."

"These genetically fabricated bodies await the transplantation of life plasm from the Andonite tribespeople. The moment these one hundred assistants step into their new forms, they will be tuned into our life circuits. The operation itself is scheduled to commence in exactly ten days from today."

Karl exchanged a brief, assessing glance with Lucifer, then stated, "Sir, you must expedite your report. Lucifer's time is short."

Caligastia took a long, measured breath, his voice imbued with the weight of destiny. "Once our one hundred Andonite assistants have graduated from our schools, they will be promptly returned to their tribes. A new hundred will then be selected, receive their life circuit implants, and be integrated into our educational program. This cycle will repeat indefinitely, ensuring the steady evolution of our subjects."

Before Caligastia could advance further in his explanation, Lucifer offered nothing more than a silent nod of approval. Then, with an elegant and deliberate gesture, he raised an arm high, summoning his high-flying seraphic transport.

Within the span of a few seconds, the transport hovered fifty feet overhead. Without any formal farewell, an intense beam of radiant energy engulfed Lucifer and just as suddenly as he had appeared, he was gone. In rapid succession, another transport descended from the sky, paused momentarily, and then, in another burst of fleeting energy, the quartet of officials vanished as well.

Caligastia, with a measured calm born of countless such encounters, ambled to the center of the expansive field, turning slowly to drink in the panoramic vista: a budding forest gently bowed before the sands of the ocean bay, while the rhythmic, timeless crashing of gulf waves on the beach filled the air with a hypnotic lullaby. "What a glorious sight and sound," he sighed deeply. "This is undoubtedly the most beautiful region in the world, if not all of Radania."

CHAPTER 8

Lisa and Don walked into the illuminated surgical room at the Planetary Center of Art and Science, where an expanse of hospital-like beds stretched wall-to-wall. Resting on each bed were one hundred Andonite tribespeople, the finest strains of that unique race, lying unconscious with transfusion devices clinging to their arms and chests. Hovering above them, circular transparent spheres pulsed with electrifying crackles that painted the air with flickering light.

Don and Lisa were monitoring the Andonites' status when a sudden high-pitched noise heralded the arrival of visitors to Earth. "The commission from Gallon," Lisa said with a sigh of relief that mingled with the steady hum of machines. "Finally, we can begin the transfusion and implantation process. I'm anxious to get this over with."

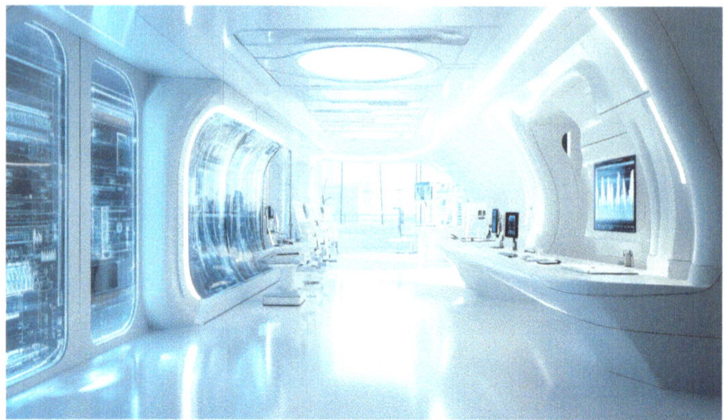

Together, they navigated briskly toward a sleek white metallic door at the far end of the room. "I'm curious about how this technique works," observed Don, his voice low with intrigue. "We've read about it in class, but witnessing an actual life circuit implantation along with a live plasm extraction is a rare opportunity."

As they waited by the transportation module to welcome their guests, a profound zooming sound was soon joined by a soft, deliberate thud that gently shook the building, clear indications that the shuttle had arrived.

"Well, you would think that, Don," Lisa said with a forced smile, pressing the button to open the shuttle's door. "I'm a bit squeamish about the whole thing; the notion of tampering with human brains just does not excite me."

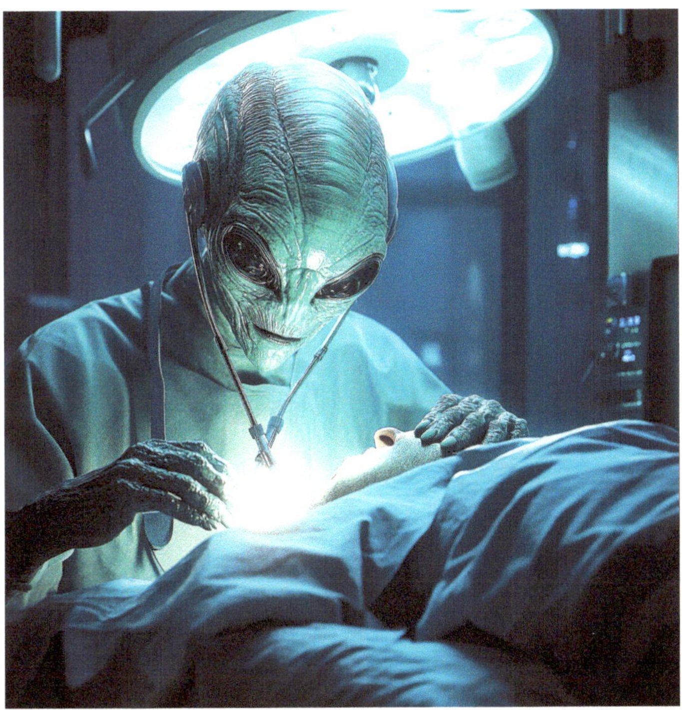

Eight beings stepped out of the shuttle and, without hesitation, split into pairs, gliding gracefully across the room towards the beds to examine their patients. Each stood about six feet tall, with the surgeons draped in crisp, sterile gowns while their assistants adorned no exterior coverings, their sexless forms bathed in the sterile light.

As the beings began their work, it appeared as though they received silent directives, seamlessly navigating from one bed to another with an efficiency that left no room for human interference. They seemed entirely indifferent to the presence of Don or Lisa. Lisa was internally awed by the formidable expertise of these extraterrestrial surgeons.

When one of the Gallon doctors initiated the implantation procedure, the energy emanating from the levitating spheres increased dramatically, sending rippling electrical currents into the dormant minds of the Andonites. Simultaneously, another doctor skillfully extracted human plasm with the aid of precision transfusion machines, channeling the vital fluid into sealed, sterile containers.

The entire procedure unfolded in just a few minutes, leaving the comatose tribespeople untouched on the surface while undergoing profound changes at a cellular level.

Ever the meticulous recorder, Don retrieved a recording devise from his backpack and began transcribing every noteworthy detail. Then, recalling the latest dispatch, he turned to Lisa with a spark of mischief. "I just received notification of Caligastia's staff assignments. Guess who's on it."

Lisa's eyes widened, her voice quivering with both anticipation and apprehension. "I can't imagine we'd know anyone on that list," she replied, secretly hoping Don's comment referred to himself. "Being considered for a position on his staff is a very prestigious honor."

Don looped his arm around Lisa's shoulder and whispered, "Our friend Mendal."

Lisa's reaction was immediate; she pulled away, her expression one of shock and disbelief. "What!" she exclaimed, glancing around to ensure her outburst hadn't disturbed the precise movements of the surgeons. "He wasn't even ready for his assignment with us."

Suppressing a wry chuckle, Don continued. "Not only that, but he's also been appointed third in command, directly below Hammone."

Lisa's face fell into a deep frown as she muttered, almost inaudibly, "This is very serious . . . something is terribly wrong. Mendal can't handle an assignment of that magnitude, he's too inexperienced. Honestly, even I would be a better third in command."

With a subtle gesture for silence, Don motioned for Lisa to focus on the intricate, delicate procedures unfolding before them. As the soft hum of machines blended with the resonant crackles of energy from the levitating spheres, Lisa's mind raced with concern and determination: she resolved to delve deeper into this unsettling development.

CHAPTER 9

Caligastia strode into the expansive recovery room of the Planetary Health and Life Center. On sleek, high-tech hospital beds, stretched out in organized rows, laid fifty meticulously engineered male and fifty equally flawless female superhumans; bodies crafted to perfection, each contoured with symmetry and precision. With an authoritative air, Caligastia addressed the nurse directly. "How did the surgical procedures go?"

"Perfectly," the nurse replied, extending a neatly organized briefcase toward him. "The staff, your third in command included, are now fully rematerialized in their newly constructed bodies. They are intricately attuned to the life circuits of the system, with the life plasm of the tribespeople now coursing through their veins. In a short while, they will awaken with full use of their superior bodies."

Caligastia's eyes narrowed inquisitively. "And what of the one hundred Andonite tribespeople? Where are they now?"

"They have completely recovered from last week's delicate operation," the nurse explained. "Though the initial awakening and exposure to the life circuits was quite a shock, they were managed with the utmost care and compassion. As we speak, they are touring Dalamatia."

Caligastia scanned the room, as if looking for someone. "Has Hammone, my second in command, arrived?" Caligastia called out to the nurse. "He's late. I wanted him here to personally inspect the staff before they become conscious. But it's too late for that now."

"Yes, sir, he just arrived," the nurse replied as he walked out of the room.

***

Later, as dusk deepened outside his office window, Hammone's nerves visibly twitched the moment the heavy door swung open. Caligastia entered accompanied by three imposing subordinates, their brisk steps echoing in the quiet room.

With a wary tone, Hammone began, "I have been meaning to speak with you, Caligastia." His eyes flickered nervously toward the others before he added, "In private."

"Anything you need to say to me can be said in front of my aides," Caligastia replied sharply, his voice laced with restrained anger that made the room feel suddenly colder.

Hammone's fingers fidgeted with unease as he carefully broached the subject. "I have reviewed the staff assignments thoroughly and I must express my concern regarding one of them. A significant concern."

"And what, may I ask, could that 'concern' be?" Caligastia inquired, his tone businesslike yet harsh enough that his aides instinctively took a step back.

"I have an objection to the appointment of Mendal as third in command. He lacks the necessary experience, training and—"

Before Hammone could complete his sentence, Caligastia's voice boomed with fury. "You, Hammone, should concern yourself with your own assignments and responsibilities!" he thundered. "You arrived late and then neglected to report immediately to your supervisor! And that is me, Hammone, in case you have forgotten! I run this operation and take orders only from Lucifer! Is that clear?"

"Yes, sir," Hammone answered, his voice barely audible as he struggled to justify himself. "I just haven't met with Mendal yet and I was concerned that he might not be ready for his duties. When I do meet him, I will evaluate his capabilities thoroughly and report my findings to you, sir."

Caligastia's anger began to subside as he interjected coolly, "I have already assessed him." His eyes darted towards Mendal, silently instructing him to step forward. "He arrived early. Mendal, meet your supervisor."

Obediently, Mendal stepped up as instructed. With a look of startled embarrassment, Hammone reached out, offering a conciliatory handshake in apology. However, Mendal's expression remained inscrutable as he declined the gesture. His steady gaze, fixed squarely on Hammone, showed no hint of emotion.

Caligastia thumped Mendal hard on the back. "Let's see how long it takes for you to replace him." The remark drew a ripple of chuckles from the group as they exited the room together.

CHAPTER 10

Lisa blinked away the lingering remnants of sleep as she forced herself out of bed, every step pulling her further from the warmth of her covers. Her groggy eyes glanced toward the glowing digital clock on her nightstand. The harsh blue glow announced 8:00 a.m. Frustration tightened her features as she shook her head and trudged toward the bathroom for a revitalizing morning shower.

Sharp insistent raps sounded at the front door, echoing through the quiet early-morning stillness and sending a jolt of alarm throughout her body. She spun around and glanced once more at the clock before raising her voice, "Who is it?"

"Your chauffeur, ma'am," came a firm and measured reply from beyond the door, the tone laced with unyielding authority. "I was informed you'd be expecting my arrival."

"At eight in the morning?" Lisa replied, her annoyance mingling with confusion.

"Yes, ma'am," the voice repeated calmly. "I'm here to accompany you to Lucifer's private transport. You are scheduled to discuss the correspondence."

"The correspondence?" she echoed, her mind racing.

"You dispatched a personal communication to Lucifer at precisely 18:02 hours yesterday, ma'am," explained the voice methodically. "He wishes to discuss its contents with you in person."

A chill of anxiety crept over Lisa. *How could he have received it so swiftly?* The question ricocheted through her mind as she hesitated, frozen for a moment in uncertainty about her next move.

"Now, ma'am," prompted the now-impatient voice from outside.

Her mounting anxiety transformed abruptly into unadulterated fear. Clutching a sense of urgency, Lisa left the comforting confines of her bathroom and hurried toward the front door. "You'll have to wait a few minutes outside while I prepare," she blurted, her tone flustered as she attempted to compose herself. "This is all a complete surprise."

"Yes, ma'am," the voice replied.

A scant fifteen minutes later, now fully dressed in an ensemble befitting an audience with the System Sovereign, Lisa reached for the life circuit communicator perched on her desk. Drawing in a silent breath and summoning her innate psychic energy, she projected her thoughts to Don. *Don, pick up,* she implored.

"Lisa, what is it?" came Don's measured voice after a brief pause.

"I'm sorry for calling so early," she whispered, her tone barely audible as she shielded her trembling hand over the communicator. "I sent a personal communication to Lucifer regarding my concerns about Mendal's promotion. I said that someone is making a grave error. Mendal is not ready for that level of responsibility."

"You should expect to hear back from his staff within a week or so," Don replied.

"Don, I sent that message only ten hours ago," she said with a tremor of mounting fear, her voice cracking. "Now his chauffeur is at my door," she whispered urgently. "Lucifer has requested a personal meeting. That never happens, Don."

There was a pause, heavy with unspoken worries. "No, it doesn't," Don agreed after a moment. "What else did you include in the letter, Lisa?"

A hesitant whisper escaped her lips. "I knew I shouldn't have —"

"What did you say?" he pressed.

"I was angry," she admitted in a low, anguished tone. "I said that I am more qualified than Mendal."

"Lisa, what exactly did you tell him?"

Her confession tumbled out in a startled rush, "I told him I was sending a copy of the correspondence to Michael of Nebadon, but I didn't really mean it, Don. I only wanted to prove how serious I was."

Before Don could respond, the voice outside sharpened to a venomous directive: "Ma'am, if you do not come out now, I am coming in!"

"Yes, yes, just one more minute," she shouted desperately through the door. Then, quieter and more fearful, she urged, "Don, what should I do? Should I . . . Don, are you there?" But the line was dead. Lisa's hands began to tremble uncontrollably as she walked the short distance to the door and cautiously opened it.

Standing before her was an imposing figure, a seven-foot-tall human form fully encased in a glistening metallic shell. "Who, or what, are you?" she demanded, her eyes widened in disbelief.

"I act only under Lucifer's direct orders," the machine-like voice intoned. "We must depart immediately." They disappeared in a beam of energy.

***

In what felt like a disjointed dream, Lisa fidgeted with a delicate button on her blouse. However, a sudden sound, defying location as if emerging from nowhere, drew her attention, prompting her to straighten abruptly. With a resigned sigh, she retrieved a compact mirror and a hairbrush from her handbag and began combing her hair for what must have been the third time in the past half hour. *How long have I been here? Three hours? Four? she wondered.* The passing of time had lost all meaning.

The room she occupied was sparse and unfurnished, save for a sleek black leather couch upon which she was seated. The walls, painted in a dull grayish brown, were completely bare and not a single adornment hung from the ceiling. Although the space was suffused with a steady, almost otherworldly light, Lisa could not determine its source. It seemed as if the very walls themselves emitted this eerie glow.

Determined to reclaim control, she stood and declared resolutely, "I'm leaving." Perhaps her meeting had been canceled, an unannounced change that rendered her wait futile. She took three tentative steps forward but then halted abruptly, her eyes scanning the room in sheer astonishment.

The door through which she had entered was gone, there was no sign of it! The sole remaining door bore the carved inscription "System Sovereign." She reached for the doorknob, but a realization struck her: no one ever enters that room uninvited. Her eyes widened, haunted by the feeling of being observed.

An unsettling sensation crept over her, as if she were detached from her body, giving the environment a surreal vibe. As she pivoted to return to the desolate couch, her head began to spin wildly and in a dizzying instant, she perceived herself hurtling through an endless tunnel. A terrifying sensation of free fall overwhelmed her, as if the very fabric of the planet's atmosphere were collapsing around her. She plummeted toward a hard, unforgiving ground, feeling the crushing force of rock and clay as she descended deep into the earth.

The further she sank, the more intense the heat and pressure became, until at last she crashed down from the heights of an expansive underground cavern onto a bed of jagged red rock. The pain was excruciatingly real, a searing agony that left her breathless. *What's happening to me?* she thought in abject horror, recoiling from the overwhelming sensations.

Then suddenly, a piercing thought invaded her consciousness: *So, Lisa, I'm making a big mistake by promoting Mendal?* Lucifer's voice resonated directly in her mind, cold and accusatory.

No! That's none of my business, she protested internally, her thoughts wracked with disbelief.

You seem to believe it is, the voice countered.

Grotesque visions of anguished, tormented souls exploded before her eyes, manifesting all around her.

And you sent a correspondence to Michael of Nebadon? the voice continued, relentless.

No, I didn't! Lisa cried out within her mind.

And I'll make sure you never do, Lucifer declared ominously.

Desperate, Lisa tried to scream, but no sound emerged.

CHAPTER 11

The one hundred reconstructed staff members gathered under a radiant sky in a picturesque meadow just beyond the towering walls of Dalamatia. This was the location chosen for the inaugural organizational meeting of Earth's fledgling administrative government.

At the forefront, Hammone stood with unwavering confidence, ready to herald a new epoch in Earth's history. His eyes gleamed with determination as he addressed the assembled group. "You are the Caligastia One Hundred," he declared in a voice rich with pride. "Our mission is to seek out the most exceptional individuals from among the local tribes. We are here to train and inspire them and then return them to their people as teachers and leaders."

Stepping forward next to Hammone was third in command Mendal. His six feet seven inch height cast an imposing silhouette that overshadowed his superior; a meticulously constructed robust physique with broad muscles, brown eyes and flowing shoulder-length brown hair that framed his determined face.

In a brisk and businesslike tone, he declared, "The educators of the local tribes must be natives of their own communities and races. Only they possess the inherent respect required to secure the trust of their people. A world's culture, in the eyes of the universe, is measured by the civility of its society."

Everyone nodded in agreement, obviously impressed with Mendal's presence and demeanor. "The pace of cultural expansion," he continued, "is determined entirely by the ability of its inhabitants to comprehend new and advanced ideas. Our objective is to transform man from a hunter to a herder, with the idea that later on he will evolve into a peaceful farmer."

"A simple beginning for the humans," Hammone added, "will be the substitution of Creator-fear for creature-fear, or ghost worship."

After an engaging half-hour lecture, Mendal meandered through the crowd, exchanging warm handshakes with many council leaders and offering heartfelt encouragement. As he prepared to rejoin the meeting, an old friend suddenly emerged from the throng. "Don? Is that truly you?" he exclaimed with genuine delight. "It's me, Mendal!"

A flicker of perplexity crossed Don's face as he replied hesitantly, "Mendal?" After a moment of uneasy silence, his voice softened: "It's good to see you, my friend." Yet there was a subdued, lifeless quality in his tone, and he quickly averted his eyes, unable to meet Mendal's.

Oblivious to the sadness cloaking his friend, Mendal embraced him enthusiastically. "Yes, here I am once again. Although, I do look rather different this time, don't I?" he chuckled. All Don could offer in reply was a slight shake of his head and a guarded, nervous smile.

Mendal's flushed face beamed with anticipation as he scanned the gathering. "Where's Lisa?" he eventually asked, his tone brimming with affection. "I've got a big hug and kiss saved just for her."

Don fidgeted uncomfortably; his reluctance to speak was evident. Finally, in a voice edged with tension, he admitted, "She's gone, Mendal. She set out to research something, and then she just disappeared."

Shock and disbelief surged within Mendal. "What! She disappeared? Nobody simply disappears!" he exclaimed, a burning anger welling up inside him. "The life circuits keep track of all spiritual entities!"

Don's eyes glistened with unshed tears as he continued in a quavering whisper, "All records of Lisa have been erased. I truly don't know what happened to her."

In a moment of fervent dismay, Mendal threw his hands into the air and grabbed Don by the shoulders, shaking him hard. "What was she researching that was so important to her?"

Overwhelmed, Don's face turned a deep shade of red. He broke away from Mendal's grasp and began to walk off. "I—I don't know, Mendal. All I know is, she was concerned, asking relentless questions, until Lucifer himself summoned her to his planet for a consultation." His voice dropped as his body slumped further. "She never came back, Mendal. I'm sorry. I've got to leave now."

With that, Don disappeared into the crowd, leaving Mendal standing motionless, his head shaking in disbelief over the heartbreaking news. Consumed by the mysterious fate of Lisa, he ventured into the nearby forest for a few moments of solitary contemplation.

Later, the staff gathered again for another session. Hammone resumed command while Mendal lingered at the edge of the assembly, his mind still haunted by recent events. With a resonant voice, Hammone declared, "Unique bodies of flesh and bone have been crafted for you, ensuring you resemble the Earth inhabitants. Yet, you are uniquely attuned to the life circuits of the Radania system."

A thoughtful interjection came from Hap, the leader of the college of revealed religion, "Is there not a danger in mortals beginning to view us as gods?"

With emphatic certainty, Hammone responded, "Yes, such worship can be a serious obstacle to your influence as teachers. It is essential that you avoid resorting to supernatural methods or superhuman manipulations."

Just then, a loud rustling and crackling sound emanated from the darkened woods. The entire staff turned as one toward the forest; when the ominous sounds subsided without incident, Hammone pressed on. "During the implant process," he explained, "the mental capacity of the one hundred Andonites was significantly enhanced. They can now grasp complex concepts and engage with us intelligently. Their rigorous education and training started one week ago."

A warm smile spread across Hammone's face as he gestured toward shadowy figures emerging from the forest. "Our local friends are overflowing with curiosity about us, especially now that one hundred of them reside within the walls of Dalamatia."

Just as Hammone and Mendal began to lead the staff back toward the city, the tranquil atmosphere shattered. Dozens of tribespeople suddenly stormed from the forest, their determined expressions set as they wielded crude clubs, sharpened spears and jagged knives.

With the untamed speed of wild beasts, the first wave of attackers descended upon the staff. Clubs rained down with brutal force, striking legs, heads and bodies until they crumbled to the ground. Soon, a second group, brandishing flint knives honed to a deadly edge, emerged to slit the throats of those already lying defenseless on the blood-soaked earth.

The one hundred, unaccustomed to such ferocity, stood in paralyzed astonishment. "Run for the city walls!" Mendal roared in a voice thick with thunderstruck urgency. "Do not stop, flee now!"

As chaos reigned, Hammone focused his mind and activated the emergency transport beams designed to whisk them to safety. But the assault was relentless. Flint-tipped arrows shot from the treetops whistled through the air, tearing through one defenseless body after another. In a heart-wrenching moment, a dozen staff members fell, their agonized screams echoing across a savage, untamed world.

Driven by desperation, Mendal sprinted to a fallen colleague, hoisting her limp form as he raced toward the towering wall. Along his frantic path, he encountered another colleague with two arrows embedded in his body. Torn between the instinct to rescue yet another friend and the desperate need for self-preservation, he hesitated. Tribespeople leaped from behind trees and, with swift precision, they drew their arrows, aimed intently at Mendal and fired.

At that very instant, Mendal and his remaining comrades were enveloped by a brilliant beam of energy that transported them to the safety of the city. One by one, the staff vanished into the beam until not a single body remained.

The tribespeople, led by Almed, a tall, thin man with deep red skin and long black hair, rushed the city fortress. Scaling the forty-foot walls an impossible task, Almed grouped together his warriors to celebrate their successful attack. They shrieked and whooped, throwing rocks and spears at the city walls.

The victory festivity lasted several hours and was attended by women and children of the surrounding tribes. Later in the afternoon, storm clouds gathered, thunder crackled and driving rain whipped through the swarm of tribespeople, bring an end to their revelry.

From behind the protective walls of Dalamatia, Mendal absorbed the somber truth: this brutality marked the end of his people's naive way of life. Unaccustomed to the savage methods of native Earth beings, he sensed that stormy, turbulent times lay painfully ahead.

CHAPTER 12

The morning after the massacre, seventy remaining staff members, along with their assistants, assembled in the expansive city courtyard at the temple of the Unseen Father for their morning prayer. Hammone and Mendal stood together beneath the boughs of a magnificent fruit-bearing tree, a recent gift from the Most Highs.

Under the shelter of the Tree of Life, Hammone led the prayer, his voice resonant with reverence. As the prayer ended, Mendal's eyes lingered on the tree. "Observe," he remarked, "its massive upper branches swoop gracefully toward the heavens, as if to receive a gift from God, while its lower branches droop humbly to present that gift to the people of Earth."

Inquisitively, Fad, the scholarly leader of the Faculty of Knowledge, said, "I always thought the Tree of Life was merely a legend. What wonders might it bestow on us here on Earth?"

Drawn in by its mythic allure, the staff stepped forward and gently touched the tree's shimmering leaves, gnarled branches and the apple-like fruit suspended among them. "I have been told," Hammone intoned with a rare intensity, "that consuming the fruit of the Tree of Life releases the universe's very life-extension force. This superfruit gathers potent energies from space itself, halting the ravages of aging."

Cradling a piece of the divine fruit, Mendal explained, "Your trepidation is entirely justified. When the Most Highs learned of our tragedy, they swiftly sent us this extraordinary tree. Those who partake in its fruit will not only cease to age but will become invincible, utterly incapable of dying a mortal death."

With deliberate conviction, Mendal bit into the fruit, leaving the crowd awestruck. A radiant smile spread across his face as he savored a second bite and struck a pose of bold invincibility, prompting gentle smiles of approval from those around him.

"Our lost friends," said Hammone, turning the crowd's attention back to himself, "sadly will not return. However, this was their choice as a group. Their replacements are being processed as we speak and will be ready to assume responsibilities by tomorrow."

Beth, the head of the council on food and material welfare, stepped up to the tree and carefully plucked a piece of fruit. "But what if tribespeople were to eat this fruit?" she inquired cautiously. "Would they too become immortal?" Nods of consensus rippled through the crowd.

"The fruit," Mendal clarified, "holds no special benefit for ordinary Earthlings. However, for any of you and your assistants, who have the life circuits flowing within your veins, it will extend your mortality indefinitely." A collective sigh of relief passed among the staff.

Mendal continued, "However, be forewarned; the benefits will gradually diminish if you cease consuming the fruit." Gesturing invitingly toward the ancient tree, he added, "You may now freely partake of the fruit of the Tree of Life." In an orderly procession, each staff member and assistant approached to claim their share of this celestial bounty.

CHAPTER 13

J en, the head of the council on art and science, chatted with a few of her friends. She had fair skin, cobalt blue eyes and long red hair. Close by her side was her tribe assistant Han. He was six feet six inches tall with long blond hair and chiseled facial features.

"I feel so much better now that the Most Highs have shown their support by sending this tree," Jen said to Han, wanting to get to know

him better. After a few moments of silence, she spoke again. "You were the only one chosen from your tribe, Han. This is a great privilege. You must feel honored."

Han smiled shyly and nodded.

"How's your schooling? Are you overwhelmed?" she asked warmly.

"No," said Han, his eyes widening with excitement, "everything is so different after the operation." He paused and looked at the ground for a moment before continuing. "But I feel comfortable with my new life."

An associate behind them asked Jen a question on science. When she finished, she turned back to Han. "How do you feel about the horrible attack yesterday, Han?" Jen asked. She needed to know if he suffered any lingering effects from the day before. "That was the worst thing I've ever experienced."

"Truthfully, I expected it. I was once one of them," Han said with a deep sigh. "But now . . ." He smiled coyly and modestly turned away.

"Please go on, Han," encouraged Jen. "You can talk to me about anything."

Han took a deep, relaxing breath. "I know I am here to learn. Then I can return to my people and teach them."

"You've already learned a lot, and quickly, Han," said Jen with respect.

He gently touched her hand and she took his and held it tightly for a moment.

"When you return to your people and take a partner, your children will have your increased intelligence and access to the life circuits," Jen explained, her face beaming. "That way, generation after generation, all of Earth's tribes will gradually progress to a higher spiritual level. This process happens everywhere in the universe."

Their names were called, and they stepped up to eat the fruit of the tree of life.

As the midday heat softened into a gentle warmth, Mendal and his tribal assistant Fay rested leisurely beneath the outstretched branches of the magnificent tree. Mendal gazed at Fay with tender admiration, marveling at her natural, earthen beauty. Slender and standing an impressive six feet tall, she possessed long, flowing dark brown hair, a naturally tanned complexion and a pair of brown eyes with a striking violet hue.

"Fay," he said kindly, "your people have experienced a remarkable beginning on Earth. Yet now, your civilization must evolve in order for your tribes to ascend to a higher level." He paused. "What do the Andonites think of us?" Mendal could sense, at least he hoped, that Fay was about to let down her guard and open up to this visitor from space.

"The belief of most of my people is that you and the others are the gods that created Earth," Fay said, "and have come to inspect your creation." She brushed her long hair from her face and leaned back against the great tree.

Mendal knelt beside her and gently put his hand on her shoulder, wanting her to feel comfortable enough to continue.

With a voice tinged both with concern and resolve, Fay replied, "They fear that you might not approve of us and could even destroy everything to start over."

Mendal looked deeply into Fay's eyes and, for a moment, he became lost in her beauty and earthly elegance.

"The fear among my people," she said, her voice quavering, "is at times overwhelming for them. It can turn into deadly violence, as you saw yesterday."

Mendal tenderly touched Fay's face. "It's hard for them to understand that we're not here to punish," he said, "but we're here to help and teach."

Fay sighed and nodded as she and Mendal stood. "Fay, there is no natural process toward a higher mental, moral or social existence."

Fay, shaking from a sudden cool breeze, edged closer to Mendal. "Please explain more," she said softly.

"This process of uplifting primitive beings has been applied on literally millions of planets across this universe," he said. "Without our guidance and teachings, humankind would remain shackled to its archaic rituals, superstitions and natural hostilities toward others."

Fay sighed, her face slightly drawn. "All this learning is hard for me, Mendal."

Mendal spoke candidly. "And I can't promise you everything will get easier, Fay. It won't. Studying is difficult, but the rewards are worth the effort."

Suddenly aware of the passing hours, Mendal reluctantly pulled away. "I must preside over a council staff meeting this afternoon. Since you're my assistant, we will have plenty of time to explore these new ideas together."

After Mendal departed, Fay looked around at the other staffers, each paired with their assistants and engaged in quiet companionship. In that moment, even amidst chaos and transformation, there lay an opportunity for renewal and progress.

CHAPTER 14

Mendal rose early one morning, his mind still settling into the rhythm of routine a year after the arrival of the tree of life. As usual, for his first task of the day, he logged onto the computer for the latest news from the system headquarters. All he found was the standard profiles of current promotion candidates and the most recent planets being considered for life implantation, the same news that had been broadcast for the last week. "How about updating once in a while," Mendal complained to the computer.

"What's that you're saying?" questioned Fay, emerging from her bedroom in the nude, her graceful form illuminated by the sun's glow. At six feet tall, her striking beauty was impossible to ignore. With a modest hint of seduction, she dried herself and combed her hair slowly, each movement a deliberate allure.

"Just talking to myself," he replied. As third in command, he enjoyed certain privileges that kept him quietly grateful. Their life was set in a private, custom-built home nestled on the gentle outskirts of Dalamatia, a secluded retreat surrounded by nature's striking beauty.

Mendal's occasional lingering glances sparked a strange mixture of admiration and forbidden desire. He wondered if her graceful, yet deliberate display was meant to tempt him sexually. However, both were painfully aware of the strict rules governing their community and as a respected leader, he knew well that temptation was one line they dared not cross.

"I didn't hear you come in last night," Mendal remarked curiously. "Out with friends again?"

"Yes," her voice soft as she stood partly draped by a robe that did little to hide her allure. "I didn't want to wake you."

"Caligastia?"

"And others," she added with a slight smile.

Mendal couldn't help but notice the frequent mention of him, a subtle pinch of jealousy tightening his chest at the thought of her mixing with others so often.

Shifting the conversation, Fay asked, "What are the plans for to-morrow? Are we just going to slog over staff reports all day or can we try something different for a change?"

Intrigued by the prospect of breaking the tedious cycle, Mendal leaned forward. "Different? What do you have in mind?" he inquired with anticipation. "There isn't much new to do compared to what we've been doing the past few weeks."

Without hesitation, Fay blurted out, "I want to visit my family."

Her words struck him like a sudden chill. "What! You mean your tribal family?"

Fay nodded and, in that instant, a shiver traveled through her. Tears began to glisten and roll down her trembling face as she looked at Mendal with a sorrow he had never seen before.

Gently, he drew her into his arms. "You've been through seminars and counseling, Fay," he whispered with concern in his voice. "You're not the same person you once were. You're now attuned to the intricate life circuits with your mind-implants. I doubt even your own people would recognize you now." The words stung as soon as they left his lips, and he instantly regretted them.

"They'd know me, Mendal!" she cried out as she pushed him away. "My family would know me! It hasn't been that long!" Overwhelmed by grief, Fay allowed her sorrow to take over and wrapped her arms around him, clinging desperately as if to salvage some familiar comfort.

"Fay, we can't contact any tribe, not yet," Mendal said gently, reluctantly pulling away. "When your training is finished, you will return to them as a teacher, as a leader."

"I love you so much," Fay wept, her words breaking with heartache, "and I love this new life you've given me, but I need to see my family again."

"No, Fay." Mendal's voice was firm and resolute. "I cannot allow it. It's against policy and I will not violate any system directive."

"You mean you simply won't do it! You can do anything you want, Mendal, you're in charge here. You just won't do it for me!" Fay cried before she turned and fled to her bedroom, slamming the door behind her.

At midday, with a heavy heart and a troubled mind, Mendal shut down his computer and gathered the notes and materials for his lecture. As he headed out, he paused at the doorway, casting one last glance toward Fay's room. "This will be the first lecture you've missed!" he shouted into the silence. Receiving no response, he shrugged and slammed the door behind him.

***

The classroom was filled with energy as Mendal delivered his lecture; a session that spanned over an hour, culminating in a resounding standing ovation. Even as he shook hands with many members of the audience, a quiet ache lingered within him. Fay's noticeable absence was a warning sign of the fading zeal she once had for learning about God.

Turning down numerous social invitations, Mendal ambled slowly toward home, each step bringing him closer to the inevitable awkward encounter with Fay. As he rounded the final bend on his journey, a breathtaking sight captured his attention: a luminous, white object hovering above the branches of a tree across the path. It was a seraphim angel of destiny! Mendal's heart lifted at the sight and a warm smile spread across his face as he quickened his pace, eager to greet her.

As he bowed courteously before this distinguished visitor, Mendal addressed her, "I am honored by your presence, ma'am. What may I do for you?"

"We are pleased by your talk today, Mendal," she replied. "You have enlightened the Earth people about us and in turn, they will share this knowledge with their tribes. This will ease our work and for that, we are appreciative."

"Thank you, ma'am," he replied respectfully.

"But I am not here solely to offer thanks, Mendal, for you are merely performing the role for which you were designed," she continued, her words growing more grave. "I am here to relay a message from the Most Highs."

Startled, Mendal exclaimed, "What! A message from the Most Highs? What do they wish to tell me?"

"They feel profoundly about this matter, Mendal. They charge you with taking Fay back to her previous home in the forest for a visit. This act is essential, as it will set off a series of events we desire, and they insist it be executed as soon as possible."

"Why is this so important?" Mendal asked, blinking in surprise and struggling to understand. "I find it hard to believe—"

"Don't argue," the angel interjected sharply. "You have heard and understood, Mendal. My task is concluded. Now, do as you are told!" In an instant, the being vanished, leaving Mendal to grapple with the weight of her words.

No sooner had he reached the familiar door of his residence than the angel reappeared before him. "I'm sorry, Mendal, for that unfortunate outburst of mine. It appears that some critical probabilities are converging on Earth soon and you are deeply involved. You must take Fay to her home in the forest without delay. If you do not, disaster will be unleashed. Remember, I and the other seraphim stand ready to help, whatever may arise."

Mendal nodded as the angel vanished once more. He stepped inside his residence and there he found Fay waiting for him with open arms.

CHAPTER 15

Mendal and Fay stepped cautiously into the pulsating heart of her ancestral tribal village, where every rustle of leaves and crackle of the distant campfire felt amplified.

As they approached, a low, smoky haze curled around the trees, carrying the scent of charred wood and venison. In the center of the clearing, ten tribespeople gathered closely around a blazing pit fire. They worked quickly, slicing freshly slain deer for the evening meal.

At the mere sight of Mendal, the atmosphere tensed. With animalistic intensity in their eyes, they closed ranks and gathered themselves into a defensive formation, circling around him while clutching flint-tipped spears and rugged knives.

The women wore light clothing while the men wore weathered buckskin that revealed powerful muscles honed by survival. The children hid behind gnarled trees and within the cool recesses of rock cliff caves that had sheltered them for generations. Although they recognized Fay, their eyes filled with hesitant fear kept them concealed in the shadowy fringes of the gathering.

"We're unharmed," Fay reassured them in her native tongue, her voice trembling. No elder answered her, yet a lone child, tears streaming down his dirt-smudged face, cried out her name and made a frantic dash toward her, only to be held back by a protective mother.

"Do not fear these visitors from the sky," Fay continued, her words choked with emotion as she tried to steady her voice. "They have come to ease our burdens, I promise you."

Dani Tribespeople, Indonesia

The tribespeople varied greatly in stature, some under five feet six inches, others towering above six feet. Their raw, primal demeanors nearly intimidated Mendal, even though his own body was conspicuously larger and more robust.

In unison, the gathered men began to emit low grunts, each thumping their spear against the earth as a signal, a summons that beckoned others from the depths of the forest. Among them emerged Almed, the formidable tribal leader, his presence a silent command over the restless crowd.

"Father," Fay pleaded softly, her voice wavering, "all that I learn, I will pass on to you. Together, we will find strength." But her words fell on deaf ears; Almed and the tribe's warriors locked their predatory stares on Mendal, their numbers swelling.

Tears cascaded down Fay's face as she gazed tenderly at the children. "The youth of our tribe can learn, just as I am learning. These gods from the sky," she said, glancing pointedly at Mendal, "they can show us new ways to hunt, to grow food, to defend ourselves."

Dani Tribespeople, Indonesia

Yet even her heartfelt appeal received no acknowledgment, not even from her own father. Turning directly to Mendal with frustrated resolve, Fay said, "I'm getting nowhere with you here. My people are afraid of anyone who is not one of them."

The men of the tribe gathered up clubs and rocks, whispering among themselves before vanishing silently into the embracing darkness of the forest.

"The only way they might listen, might be willing to explore these new ideas, is if I appear alone," Fay insisted, her voice shrill with desperation. "Then, perhaps, they will give us a chance." Mendal could only nod, his attention ever drawn to the shifting activity behind them.

"I will return later," she whispered, "and try to explain to them who you are, and why you have come." Slowly and solemnly, Fay and Mendal backed away from the light of the campfire.

Once enveloped by the forest's cool, shadowed embrace, they began the somber trek home. The hush between them was broken only by

Fay's soft, choking sobs. "They couldn't find the courage to speak with me, Mendal, not even my own family."

Mendal squeezed her hand in a quiet promise, though his senses remained on high alert as he caught the faint sound of footsteps and the rustling of leaves around them. His muscles coiled instinctively, adrenaline surging through him like electric currents, while his mind struggled to fathom the unfolding peril.

"Sometimes," Fay said wistfully, "I wish that none of this pain had ever found me."

Before the lingering melancholy could settle, a sudden eruption of movement startled them. Six tribesmen burst out from the woodland shadows, brandishing spears, clubs and stones with the ferocity of threatened beasts.

Unarmed, Mendal faced them as Fay screamed, her cry ringing out in the tense air. "I come in peace," Mendal declared, his voice firm despite the hammering in his chest. "I am a friend of Fay." He clung to the ancient Tree of Life legend as he scooped up Fay, instinctively positioning himself as her wall against the impending storm. Terrified, Fay shrank close to the ground, her body trembling.

In a whirlpool of savagery, the tribesmen pounced with the unrelenting ferocity of wild animals. Spears, thrown with lethal precision, found their way to Mendal's chest. He tore them out with fierce determination even as the jagged, flint-tipped points clawed at him, ripping his flesh. Yet not a drop of blood flowed, and no pain pierced his consciousness, just as the ancient legends had promised.

The brutality escalated. Two tribesmen sprang onto Mendal from behind, pinning him with brute force as Almed seized a fistful of his hair and yanked his head back with savage intensity. With a swift, merciless slash, Almed's twelve-inch knife sliced halfway through Mendal's neck; the wound closed with an almost supernatural speed, leaving only a jagged scar as testimony to its occurrence.

Suddenly, a primal burst of uncontrollable strength surged through Mendal. He broke free from his captors with astonishing ease and pivoted to confront the warriors. Tearing off a heavy branch from a nearby tree, he wreaked havoc on those who dared approach Fay. He then pulverizing two more and hurled their dying bodies against rugged rock cliffs.

In a final, chilling act, Mendal wrested a man climbing a tree to escape, snapping his neck in one fluid motion before hurling his limp body into a tree stump. Unleashed human rage transformed the clearing into a macabre scene of death and destruction.

Stunned by the monstrous force he had become, Mendal collapsed to his knees. Almed and the remaining men withdrew into the forest's depths. In the distance, Fay's harrowing shriek echoed as Mendal fought to regain control over the deluge of emotions that had overtaken him, a raw humanity he had never felt before.

Mendal staggered away to a nearby creek, his hands working feverishly to wash away the gruesome evidence; the blood, skin and bone, that clung to him. He scanned the surroundings for any sign of Fay until he spotted her, kneeling forlornly by the rock cliffs.

With careful tenderness, he lifted and carried her to a welcoming grassy knoll. There, he held her tight in a protective embrace, while she clung to him as if their souls were interwoven. "We are one now, Mendal," she whispered softly. "Let our souls merge completely, in every way possible."

Though his heart burned with an equally intense longing, Mendal restrained himself. "These feelings, no matter how powerful, are forbidden by the guidelines set by the Most Highs," he said, gently laying her down amidst the tall, swaying blades of grass. Sitting beside her, he fought to subdue the animalistic yearning stirring within him.

Fay's passion overflowed. "I am no longer bound by the old ways," she breathed into his ear, her voice sultry and provocative. "The life circuits course through my entire being and my very blood dances in your veins." Her hands roamed over him, her touch both seductive and desperate. "We must not deny this connection."

Mendal paused. "We cannot, Fay. Not in the physical realm, not with raw, unchecked animal passion." With a deliberate tenderness, he stroked her forehead with his hand before drawing her close against his broad chest. Closing his eyes, he sank into a deep, meditative calm. "Before I was granted this mortal body," he whispered softly, "when I existed as a spirit bound to one whom I deeply loved, our souls would merge in a single, transcendent moment."

His soft words fueled the fire of Fay's desire. "I long to share that pleasure with you, Mendal," she whispered. As he closed his eyes, he slowly tilted his head toward the heavens, venturing mentally through the spiritual realms while his hands graced the contours of Fay's shoulders, breasts and stomach. In that otherworldly space, he reached the very core of her being, gently stimulating her inner animal spirit with his mind.

Fay's body shivered and contorted with ecstatic delight as his mental caresses descended into a frenzied rhythm. Overwhelmed by passion, she pulled him down until their bodies entwined, their forms merging in a primal act of intimacy.

With his eyes still closed in transcendent focus, Mendal continued his mental massage deep within Fay's soul. For a full, heart-pounding fifteen minutes, their union escalated into a spontaneous eruption of passion; a moment of simultaneous, explosive ecstasy that reshaped the air around them.

Collapsed and spent beneath the shade of an ancient tree, they lay in silence until Mendal suddenly sensed a peculiar, shimmering presence; a distinct spiritual energy unlike any he had previously encountered. Rising slowly, he moved to his left as a figure began to materialize out of the dense shadows. Within moments, he found himself face to face with an otherworldly creature whose features were hazy, yet whose presence was undeniable.

"What are you?" Mendal asked in an awestruck tone. "Where do you come from?"

The creature radiated a cascade of sparkling energy, its aura pulsing luminescent patterns in the dim light. "I exist on a different midway level of life-functioning and my name is Zee," the being communicated telepathically, its voice echoing softly in both Mendal's and Fay's minds.

"How is it possible that you have suddenly appeared here with us?" Mendal inquired, his eyes wide with amazement.

"Your unique spiritual lovemaking released a surge of energy that allowed me to be born upon Earth," Zee explained, his voice carrying the weight of cosmic wisdom.

Mendal and Fay exchanged looks of incredulous wonder as they witnessed this being whose features gradually sharpened. He was a tall, almost seven-feet silhouette marked by a slender upper body and shoulders with light gray skin. Fay whispered to Mendal, "Despite his immense size, there is an air of calm, almost a timid grace."

Mendal, however, could sense power beneath his exterior. "And yet his energy is anything but gentle," he said, noting the vigorous pulsing that surged in and around the creature's form.

"I am visible to you and Fay, as well as anyone connected to the life circuits," Zee continued telepathically, "but be assured, I cannot be seen by the human tribes."

"Are you telling us that you can move about our world undetected?" Mendal asked, his voice brimming with astonishment.

"Yes," Zee replied simply. "There are many among us awaiting our release. We are here to serve the prince's administration through our ability to study and observe the diverse races of this world remotely located from the planetary headquarters."

At last, as the sun dipped beneath the horizon, Mendal and Fay started their journey home. And Zee went with them.

CHAPTER 16

"Fay, we're late!" Mendal called out, his voice echoing down the silent corridor as it reached the closed bedroom door.

Fay emerged slowly, her presence immediately captivating in a low-cut, sky-blue gown that clung elegantly to her form. The delicate fabric shimmered softly in the morning light, drawing attention to her full, conspicuous curves. "Well, dear, we wouldn't be late if you hadn't decided, at the very last minute, to try and create another creature," she replied with a playful, bewitching smile. "We didn't quite succeed this time, but nice try."

Mendal's laughter, warm and teasing, filled the air as they strode out into the hallway. "Then we will simply have to try again tomorrow," he added with a glimmer of hope.

***

Inside Caligastia's lavishly decorated banquet hall, Mendal's nervous energy was noticeable as he turned to Fay, who sat gracefully beside him at one of the circular dining tables. The room shimmered with intricate detailing, its walls and ceilings adorned with lavish designs that commanded awe. "And I thought we were late," Mendal whispered, his voice anxious. "Here we are, Fay, alone with Zee while everyone's glares at us."

The grand double doors swung open, revealing Lucifer, Satan and three dignified Planetary Princes. They entered with an air of regal authority, each step measured and graceful. The room fell into a hush as every guest watched them in respectful silence until polite applause broke the tension.

Lucifer, dressed impeccably in a black tuxedo trimmed in gold, exuded an aura of danger wrapped in elegance. His hair was swept back into a tight ponytail, and his gloved hands, as black as midnight, added to his sharp presentation. He removed his full-length, sleek black coat with a flourish and tossed it to one of the princes, his smile broad and confident, a look that seemed to command both respect and adoration.

"I've never seen Lucifer like this," Mendal whispered to Fay. "He actually smiled and for him to acknowledge the presence of his underlings? It's unprecedented."

Fay's eyes, deep and knowing, locked onto Lucifer as if trying to decipher the layers beneath his exterior. "Lucifer has always championed the common, hard workers," she said softly. "He cares for us and will go to any lengths for our sake." Mendal, preparing to respond, was interrupted as Lucifer and his entourage approached their table.

In unison, Mendal, Fay and Zee stood up in a respectful gesture. Once Lucifer took his commanding position at the head of his table, the entire assembly resumed their seats, their collective gazes fixed on him. Yet, unlike the others, Lucifer remained standing, his piercing steel-gray eyes sweeping across the chamber with an intensity that seemed to penetrate the very souls of the onlookers.

Soon, Caligastia, accompanied by Hammone, ascended the winding, grand staircase and positioned himself behind an elaborately carved podium. His voice boomed through the ornate hall. "We gather today to formally announce the introduction of the midway creatures, beings that exist in the unique space between the mortal and the angelic realms."

His statement created a respectful hush among the gathered guests. "The Most Highs have granted us unprecedented permission to usher these new creatures into the Earth dimension. With the collaborative efforts of Mendal and Fay," Caligastia continued, "we shall initiate supermaterial liaisons between all male and female staff associates and their assistants. Our ambition is to bring forth as many of these ethereal beings as possible."

Promptly, the staffers erupted into applause, enthusiastic and laden with anticipation, each individual eager to explore the promise of this bold new phase of physical intimacy. Applause from the group didn't subside until Zee stood. "I would like to commend Mendal for finding a way to bring me into existence in your time-reality," Zee communicated humbly. Everyone smiled.

Amidst this fervor, Satan rose, his mere presence arresting the room. Mendal had always admired Satan's commanding appearance; a robust, strapping figure with white hair and beard, his strong physique complimented by weathered, leathery skin and penetrating eyes that seemed to see everything.

As soon as Satan cleared his throat, a hush fell over the room like a heavy curtain descending upon all chatter. Mendal was utterly mesmerized by his imposing presence. *Is it just me or does every word he speaks leave everyone spellbound?* he silently wondered.

"I am pleased to announce," Satan began, "that the midway creatures will serve as the intelligence corps of Caligastia's grand administration. We will rigorously train these midway creatures at our system headquarters before assigning them to various esteemed Planetary Princes in Radania."

Satan gestured for Mendal to rise and accept acknowledgement. Mendal hesitated but encouraged by Fay, stood. "I also commend Mendal for researching such a fascinating subject," said Satan with a gleam in his eye. "He may now be third in command at Dalamatia, but if he keeps up this kind of performance, he will rapidly advance to universe administration."

Lucifer acknowledged Mendal with a dignified nod. He raised his arms in a splendid, almost theatrical gesture and, in a brilliant burst, he evaporated in a cascade of radiant light, ascending to his personal seraphic transport that awaited him.

Mendal leaned close to Fay. "Lucifer certainly adores the spotlight. I've heard rumors that every event turns into a stage for him, where he's the sole star; self-love incarnate."

Fay's eyes flickered with disapproval as she glanced at him. "Be cautious with your words, Mendal," she hissed softly. "Remember, he is our System Sovereign and our respect for him must be unwavering." Mendal, pretending not to register her caution, wandered off to mingle with his fellow staff members.

CHAPTER 17

Later, as Caligastia readied himself for departure, he noticed Satan standing adjacent to him. Satan's eyes, vivid and predatory, locked onto him. "What is it, sir?" Caligastia inquired.

"We need to talk immediately, in private," Satan replied tersely, his lips curving with barely concealed intensity. The two men moved briskly into Caligastia's private office, a room dominated by massive video screens that enveloped all four walls, each displaying scenes from different sectors of the universe.

Leaning against his dark mahogany desk, Caligastia attempted to mask his unusual nervousness, his mind racing with questions about this surprising summons from Lucifer's formidable second in command. "We are preparing to announce, publicly and without delay, our intent to liberate the system of Radania from the oppressive clutches and control of Michael of Nebadon," Satan declared in a brisk tone that filled the room with tension. Caligastia's face turned a pale shade of shock as his eyes widened in disbelief.

Satan motioned for Caligastia to take a seat. "At present, we have secured the backing of thirty-seven Planetary Princes," Satan thundered, his words echoing off the polished surfaces. "We expect Earth to be the pivotal thirty-eighth." Despite the turmoil in his mind, Caligastia managed to settle into a chair at the foot of his desk.

"In the vast expanse of the ten thousand systems that make up Nebadon," Satan continued, his voice forceful, "there have been only two rebellions and both crumbled, for the masses largely failed to follow their Planetary Prince."

With a tremor barely restrained, Caligastia ventured, "How can I be certain that this rebellion will not falter like those previous debacles?"

Satan's energy surged, practically knocking Caligastia off balance with the force of his conviction. "Lucifer will succeed," he proclaimed with ringing certainty, "where others have faltered because he will have the allegiance of the majority of planets in Radania. 'Majorities rule' will be our rallying cry in this grand revolution!"

Seeking a moment of reflection, Caligastia rose and approached a wall monitor. After deftly adjusting the controls, he turned back to face Satan. "I believe," he began, "as does Lucifer, that the Universal

Father is nothing more than a myth contrived by the Paradise Sons. A myth to justify their dominion over the universes in His name. I fully support Lucifer in this revolution."

Satan's eyes flashed brightly as he bared his teeth in a snarl. "Your support means absolutely nothing," he retorted, "if the majority of the Earth's personalities do not rally behind your lead." With a sudden, forceful slam of his fist onto the mahogany table, a deep crack reverberated through the wood. Caligastia, unable to meet Satan's burning gaze, turned away.

Drifting towards a large window, Caligastia gathered his courage and finally spoke softly, his back still turned to Satan. "What, then, prevents Michael of Nebadon from quashing this insurrection entirely?" His words hung in the air like a fragile challenge against an unyielding storm.

Satan's fury flared visibly. He advanced with deliberate steps, his hands tightening into fists so fiercely that crimson droplets began to seep from his palms, staining the floor beneath. In one fluid motion, he extended a blood-drenched hand, gripped Caligastia's shoulder and spun him around to face his wrath. "Michael holds no authority over a System Sovereign such as Lucifer, because He has not yet completed His bestowal career!" he roared.

The Andromeda Galaxy

With a dramatic sweep of his arm toward the front video monitor, the screen instantly transformed into a detailed overview of the Radania system. "Until then," Satan continued, "if a majority of people choose to follow a System Sovereign in rebellion against Michael, that Sovereign shall have the power to forge his own government in any shape he desires."

Caligastia's eyes locked with Satan's, a silent clash of determination passing between them. Breaking the tense silence, Satan's tone softened as he revealed his next crucial intelligence. "To emphasize Earth's critical importance to our movement, I have received highly classified information about the location of Michael's bestowal planet. And that planet, my friend, is Earth."

Stunned into silence, Caligastia trembled as he absorbed the weight of the revelation. "Out of the millions of spheres to become mortal," he managed to whisper, "He has chosen my planet Earth?"

"If Lucifer gains control of the very planet designated for the final act in Michael's ascension to universal rule," Satan growled with dark intensity, "then you will be rewarded beyond your wildest dreams, Caligastia."

A surge of impending power and untold prestige swelled within Caligastia as he clenched his fist in a silent vow. "I guarantee that the majority of Earth's people will follow their prince!" he declared.

Satan's face hardened into a near-impenetrable mask as he spoke once more. "Convince the people of Earth to stand with Lucifer." Slowly, deliberately, Satan extended his arm and squeezed his fist until fresh, scarlet blood streamed freely, visibly staining Caligastia's polished boots. "If we fail in this, the Ancients of Days will not hesitate to obliterate all who stood against them."

With a heavy nod, Caligastia recognized the full, dire implications of Satan's words. Satan then sneered, snapped his fingers sharply and vanished from the room. A fleeting sigh of relief escaped Caligastia, but it was quickly replaced by dread as he noticed a new, ominous message seared into each of the four giant monitors:

"You, Caligastia, hold the fate of Lucifer in your hands. And he is well aware of this."

Chapter 18

Mendal trudged down the quiet cobblestone street toward Caligastia's secluded residence. The flickering gaslights cast trembling, ghostlike shadows across the uneven stones, amplifying the knot of unease coiled in his gut. Even before reaching his destination, instinct whispered the inevitability of what was to come.

Out of a narrow crevice between two timeworn buildings, a commanding shout pierced the quiet, "Halt! Be recognized!" A soldier emerged, towering at a formidable seven feet, swathed in a dark charcoal trench coat and hood that obscured as much as it revealed. His rigid jaw, eyes bulging with a silent ferocity and an expression as hard as carved stone startled Mendal and sent a jolt of alarm through his veins.

Recovering swiftly, Mendal barked, "I'm your superior, trooper. Lower your weapon!" He assessed the scene with a disturbing thought, *Satan's military. Already the ground troops are in play.*

The trooper's gaze was meticulous as he scrutinized Mendal. With a measured step back, he stammered, "Sorry, Sir. Didn't recognize you. Only seen your picture, Sir."

A flicker of irritation darkened Mendal's eyes as he snapped, "What are you doing? It's an hour before daybreak!" His irritation blended with disbelief at the absurdity unfolding before him.

"Orders, Sir," the trooper replied. "Keep off the streets. Everyone." After a pause, he added, "Not you, Sir."

Determined to assert his authority, Mendal pressed on, "How many soldiers came with you, trooper?"

"Two hundred, Sir," came the mechanical reply. With that, Mendal turned away, each step heavier than the last with the realization that an unavoidable calamity was fast approaching.

Just as Mendal approached Caligastia's imposing residence, the door swung open. There, standing in the doorway, was Hammone, his freshly shaven head catching the brilliance of the interior lights, which made it gleam like polished marble. With a polite nod that barely concealed the gravity of the moment, Hammone said, "Welcome. This is a monumental moment in history, Mendal."

Stepping briskly into the foyer, Mendal brushed past Hammone, his physical dominance pronounced with every deliberate movement. The air between them was thick with unspoken contempt. The two men entered Caligastia's austere office.

After an agonizing ten minutes, Caligastia emerged from a shadowed side door, carrying with him an aura of commanding presence. In one hand, he clutched a weathered leather-bound text; in the other, two elegantly rolled scrolls. "Gentlemen," he announced, "I have with me the Lucifer Declaration of Liberty. Lucifer has withdrawn Radania from the control of Michael of Nebadon."

Hammone's face, alight with fanatical zeal, flashed a look of disdain toward Mendal, while Caligastia's suspicious glare bore into him. In that moment, Mendal was haunted by memories of when he had seen Earth's probable future, a vision that had unfolded when he broke the rules and peered into what was forbidden. Had he truly seen the future or was it an illusion?

Caligastia continued, "For Radania to be truly free and independent, a majority of occupied planets must rally behind Lucifer's quest for liberty. I have decreed that Earth shall be the thirty-eighth planet to secede."

Hammone emphasized his loyalty by exclaiming, "I fully back you and Lucifer, this should have been done—."

Caligastia cut him off sharply. "I knew you'd be loyal, Hammone. I know how you think."

Mendal's voice took on a hardened edge as he inquired, "Is this final? Did you decide for the entire planet, Caligastia? Or does anyone else have a say?"

Caligastia's features tightened as he responded, "Majorities rule, Mendal. Every soul on Earth, human and spiritual alike, must choose to support either Lucifer or Michael. But it has been agreed that the decision of the three of us, alongside my one hundred staff and their one hundred assistants, will determine Earth's fate."

Caligastia paced toward Mendal with deliberate, measured steps. "The others will follow if we are united in our decision, Mendal. It's as simple as that."

Unfurling the scrolls, Caligastia ordered, "Hammone, as second in command, you will be the first to sign this affidavit swearing your loyalty to Lucifer as the god of Radania, renouncing any allegiance to Michael of Nebadon." Without hesitation, Hammone signed. Mendal's inner disdain was evident only in his barely suppressed sneer.

"Mendal," Caligastia said, extending the scroll toward him, "your turn."

Mendal turned away, refusing to lock eyes with his superior. "I want to know what I'm signing."

Caligastia's eyes narrowed over the rim of his spectacles as he countered, "I'll tell you what to sign, Mendal, then you'll do it!"

Before the tension could reach its zenith, a voice called out from an adjoining room, "I'll handle this, Caligastia." All heads turned as Lucifer entered. Graced in gray slacks and a sleek black, long-sleeved silk shirt embroidered with a golden dragon on the left chest, Lucifer radiated strength. His chest and broad shoulders hinted at power far beyond that of any ordinary man. Lucifer's slow, appraising glance swept over Mendal, his probing eyes and wry smirk cutting through the tension like a scalpel. It seemed as though he could peer deep into Mendal's soul, unmasking secrets hidden even from himself.

At Lucifer's entrance, the trio straightened with disciplined precision. With a measured step, Lucifer approached Mendal and placed a reassuring hand upon his shoulder. "Mendal, your decision is yours alone. We are not here to coerce you," he proclaimed, casting a searing look at Caligastia. "Hear me out. When men and angels assert themselves, claiming their rights, even the Ancients of Days have no power to subdue a revolution of native independence. Majorities rule, Mendal."

A defiant smile tugged at Mendal's lips as he reiterated, "Yes, majorities rule. You need the support of a majority of Radania's governing personalities to secure independence. Without my compliance, you will never have that majority."

Lucifer's eyes glittered with cold acknowledgement as he admitted, "You're right. We need your support." Caligastia and Hammone nodded in silent accord.

Gazing directly into Lucifer's eyes, Mendal's tone rang with unyielding resolve, "I can't give it, Lucifer." The words were firm and final, despite the storm that they promised to unleash.

Lucifer's expression shifted as he drew a deep, deliberate breath before locking his gaze back onto Mendal. With an insidious lilt, he growled, "Remember Lisa?"

At the mere mention of her name, Mendal's body convulsed, the constriction in his throat and the tightening in his gut betraying the storm of dread and anger brewing inside him. "What have you done to her?" he managed, his voice a mixture of fury and fragile hope.

Lucifer's reply was cool and unnervingly casual, "Not to worry, Mendal. She's safe with me. We get along just fine."

Mendal, though burning with a rage that beckoned him to strike, held himself back. His inner fury screamed to retaliate, yet reason warned that this battle was not yet to be won.

Undeterred, Lucifer continued his merciless taunt, "And your other girlfriend? Fay, isn't it? I'm saving her for Caligastia, she's not really my type, too barbaric and savage." He was clearly amused at having struck a vulnerable nerve. "But Caligastia likes them that way," he added with a derisive chuckle. Caligastia's smile wavered as he avoided Mendal's fierce gaze.

"What is the point of all this, Lucifer?" Mendal demanded.

Lucifer's reply was icy and deliberate, "The point, Mendal, is that you have the power to save them both. You could have them both and even the godship of any planet you desire, if you decide to stand with me in this revolution for freedom." With a swift gesture, Lucifer signaled his awaiting transport. "Remember, I have Lisa and I can take Fay. Save her from Caligastia, Mendal. He is capable of very unsavory acts." And then, as mysterious as he had arrived, Lucifer vanished.

Caligastia stepped forward once again, handing Mendal the scroll. "Sign, Mendal."

Drawing on deep inner reserves, Mendal stood his ground, "I'm not ready to make the decision," he declared, his voice unwavering.

For a moment, Hammone advanced as if fueled by anger, only to abruptly halt as fear overtook him.

Caligastia's tone softened unexpectedly. "That's fine, Mendal. I'll record you as officially 'undecided.' Your position and duties remain unchanged, and you will continue to reside in Dalamatia." Mendal nodded in reluctant acceptance.

With a dismissive smirk, Caligastia added, "We will report this immediately to Lucifer and Satan," and he departed with Hammone promptly following in his footsteps.

Left alone in the quiet aftermath, Mendal wrestled with the tumult of his inner conflict. The vision of what he had seen and the weight of choices yet to be made pressed upon him. *I must change what I saw,* he thought desperately. *But how? How can I possibly reshape the course of fate?*

CHAPTER 19

Heavily armed and clad in military uniforms that gleamed under the harsh light, soldiers from the system headquarters had been methodically deployed at every strategic juncture across Dalamatia. At every major junction, they had constructed makeshift checkpoints, their presence a stern reminder that travel was now strictly limited. The streets lay eerily deserted except for the orderly rows of military personnel, their boots echoing against the pavement.

Inside the cold, stark confines of the administrative headquarters, Caligastia's hand steadied the microphone as he prepared to address the assembly. With a voice that brimmed with authority, he proclaimed, "Today, I am the absolute Sovereign of Earth. As we speak, this announcement is reaching the Most Highs."

Mendal, who had long anticipated such a declaration, maintained his silence. The first reaction from his colleagues was a collective, questioning glance in his direction, as if seeking validation. His calm exterior hid the deep and seething pain that churned within him.

Without missing a beat, Caligastia plunged into the dire proclamation. "All administrative groups will now relinquish their functions and powers into the hands of Hammone as trustee, pending a complete reorganization of the planetary government."

At that moment, the heavy silence shattered into a riot of voices. Overlapping shouts of disgust and outrage erupted, swirling around the room. "Treason!" someone bellowed, while others added, "This is an outrage!" Their voices, raw and impassioned, reverberated off the cold, imposing walls.

At Caligastia's side, Hammone stepped forward assertively, his voice booming across the assembled crowd. "I now formally proclaim Caligastia 'god of Earth and supreme over all!'"

Amid this upheaval, Van emerged, a large, imposing black man who carried an air of authority that was impossible to ignore. As the acknowledged leader of the esteemed Court of Appeals, his presence commanded respect. With resolute conviction, he challenged the self-appointed usurpers: "I protest this outrage against the government of Michael of Nebadon!"

Immediately, six heavily built guards advanced toward Van, their movements precise and menacing. Yet, at the sight of Hammone's raised hand, they paused and then retreated to their original posts.

"As the director of the Court of Appeals," Van continued, punctuating his declaration with a forceful slam of his fist into an open palm, "I will personally petition Lucifer."

Caligastia raised his voice to address everyone present. "You're right, Van. We'll let Lucifer decide."

***

That evening and standing on a hastily constructed wooden podium in the courtyard of the temple of the unseen Father, Van addressed the gathered staff and assistants. "I'm sorry to announce that the rumors you have heard are true."

Wiping the sweat from his brow in a moment of vulnerability, he continued, "I've just received Lucifer's reply to my appeal. He commands us to give absolute allegiance to Caligastia and all his mandates." Taking a deep, steadying breath, Van declared, "The Lucifer rebellion has begun." A collective groan of dismay mingled with a few sporadic shouts of approval.

"We can't let Caligastia take over Earth!" shouted Ang, his fiery, copper hair punctuating every impassioned word. "Lucifer doesn't control the entire universe. He can't just take Radania for his own."

"But what are we going to do?" sighed Fad. "What can we do?"

Van pressed on with his grim announcements. "I formally indict for treason Hammone, Caligastia and Lucifer. They stand in contempt of the government of the universe of Nebadon."

Amid the charged atmosphere, Nod spoke up, his voice defiant: "Some of us sincerely believe in Caligastia. We will follow him and his mandates, no matter what you say, Van." His declaration was met by a gathering of supporters whose fiery expressions signaled readiness for any confrontation.

"We will fight to keep Earth," asserted Lut, his tone rising in fervor. "You are the betrayer, Van. You and your traitors are turning against the man who constructed this magnificent city." Nearly half the crowd now visibly sided with Lut and Nod. "Dalamatia is our capital. Leave, now!"

Lucifer's military vanguard, emblazoned with the unmistakable dragon symbol and armed to the teeth, slipped into position as a protective barrier against Michael's loyalists. The air grew heavy with the inevitability of conflict, each group bracing itself, unwilling to relent.

Under the weight of the mounting tension, Van and Mendal quietly removed themselves from the maddened crowd and crossed to the far side of the courtyard. A small band of staunch loyalists trailed behind them.

"Do we have to choose sides now?" Mia, a young female staff assistant, asked with trembling uncertainty. "What if some of us aren't sure which side to take?"

"The lines have already been drawn, Mia," Van answered softly. "This is now war in the heavens. Meetings and discussions will be held by both factions until all two hundred and three of us decide whether to follow Lucifer in rebellion or remain loyal to Michael and His government."

Placing a reassuring hand on Mia's slight, wiry shoulder, Van cautioned her, "Be careful. This is no game. The losers risk total annihilation of their spiritual essence . . . their very souls."

To those remaining with Van's faction, he leaned in and stated, "We must leave Dalamatia tonight." Casting a glance at Mendal, he received a solemn nod in return. "We'll set up camp outside the walls, a few miles to the northeast. Those who remain undecided will have to stay in the city." Amid the mingling of staff and assistants, many wandered between the two opposing groups, their hearts caught in the crossfire of indecision.

Mendal's eyes scanned the chaos in search of Fay. She was conspicuously absent from the loyalists' cluster. Spots of movement caught his attention, a pair from the dissident group striding across the courtyard toward a bustling cafe. He hurried after them and finally caught sight of Fay, animatedly conversing with several staff associates, including council heads Bon and Lut.

"Fay, I've been looking for you," Mendal said, his voice taut with tension. Grasping her arm, he urged her, "We're leaving Dalamatia with Van."

Startled, Fay jerked her arm back, her eyes widening, unwilling to seem as if she were under Mendal's control. "I'm not sure I want to leave Dalamatia, Mendal," she retorted.

Mendal stepped back in surprise. Fay continued, her voice defensive as she pressed, "All of my friends are following Caligastia," she said, nervously chewing her lower lip. "We feel passionately about Lucifer. The true leaders of Earth must now emerge," she added, her gaze darting away from Mendal as she sought support in the approving nods of her companions. "They must organize those inferior to do the work that needs to be done."

Mendal's was shocked as he absorbed her words. "I had no idea you felt this way, Fay," he muttered, recalling Lucifer's ominous threat regarding her future.

Her friends clustered around her protectively as council head Ward, his rugged looks accentuating his imposing stature, declared, "The smarter, stronger and more powerful among us bear the obligation to decide for those who are physically or mentally unfit. Personal liberty affords me the right to control any who are weaker than I, in any manner I deem fit." His words met with agreements from the majority, while a few still listened intently, weighing the merits of this new doctrine.

"Those who can prove their strength have the right to control me as they see fit," Ward continued, punctuating his claim with a hearty slap on the back from a supportive companion. "There is no moral God in the heavens who fancies the righteous. Might is right."

Nodding, Fay added softly, "The people want a powerful leader to make the crucial decisions for them. They want to be guided, even controlled, for their own good. You, Mendal, are the strongest among us. No one can defeat you."

Alarm and disbelief flared in Mendal's eyes. "What are you saying, Fay? That free will is a luxury afforded only to a select few rather than a universal right? And what about your family and friends, what will become of them?" he demanded.

"All I'm saying is that we need a chosen few to dictate what is best for the rest of us," Fay replied, tears beginning to cloud her eyes. "My family will learn to accept this new way. They won't be given a choice."

A woman beside Fay stepped forward, embracing her before addressing Mendal directly. "We want our leaders to decide where each of us belongs in society. We trust them implicitly."

All eyes in the assembly now turned to Mendal, waiting in heavy, suspended anticipation of his response. Lut, his tone both gentle and insistent, asked, "What have you decided, Mendal? We respect your guidance. Many of us will follow your lead, whether that means siding with Lucifer or remaining loyal to Michael."

Mendal simply shook his head, his gaze drifting from Fay to the expectant faces around him. Gently, he touched her arm. "Fay and I need to talk about this in private," he insisted tenderly. "Please, come home with me."

CHAPTER 20

The following morning Mendal woke with a heavy heart, his mind a whirlwind of perplexity over the events that had unfolded. He made his way to the kitchen where he found Fay, who had spent the restless night alone in her old room, her demeanor shadowed by the exhaustion of sleepless hours.

"I didn't sleep at all," he muttered, his voice thick with fatigue and disbelief. Fay paused in her task of rinsing a water glass and looked up at him; the dark, smudged shadows beneath her eyes spoke volumes of her own lost night.

Seeking clarity, Mendal went over to the computer terminal, its screen flickering with urgent messages. He read aloud the update: "As of this morning, all channels of interplanetary communication have been suspended."

With a sudden, resounding thud, he slammed his fist onto the desk, the impact echoing his inner turmoil. "The entire system of Radania is now quarantined," he continued, his voice rising in frustration, "the system circuits have been severed, and Earth has been alienated."

He rose, shaking his head in despair, and turned his gaze toward Fay. "Every group of life on the planet has found itself, without warning, tossed into isolation, completely cut off from any outside counsel," he explained, wincing as his face drained of color. "Without these system circuits, no one can escape our planet's confines or even reach out to anyone beyond Earth."

Fay's response was laced with concern. "These system circuits are the lifelines of communication and transportation, binding the entire universe together." Her voice trembled slightly. "How long before they're restored?"

Mendal, still absorbed in the relentless stream of system news broadcasts, offered no immediate answer. Then, just as suddenly as it had begun, the computer screen went dark. No more messages, no more news, no flicker of hope from the outside world. His head bowed and his shoulders slumped as the crushing silence enveloped him.

"Or will they ever be fully restored?" Fay whispered, the quiet desperation in her tone echoing the void that now seemed to stretch out before them.

"Not as long as Lucifer lives," Mendal replied with a bitter finality. "The purpose behind this quarantine is clear, to prevent the revolution's seeds from spreading into other systems. Every spiritual personality present on Earth is now forced to choose between the ways of Lucifer and the will of the Universal Father. Ultimately, Earth's destiny will be decided by a majority vote among the two hundred and three of us who govern its fate."

Stepping forward, Fay closed the space between them, enveloping Mendal in a gentle embrace. "You are influential, Mendal. Those who have yet to decide will inevitably follow your example."

Yet Mendal shook his head, his inner turmoil deepening. The truth revealed by the quantum probability computer was a secret too immense for him to bear any longer. Desperate for guidance, Mendal reached for his personal communicator and called Van. As he spoke, Fay's practiced hands eased the tension in his shoulders. "How are the staff reacting, Van?" he inquired.

"For now, most remain loyal to Caligastia," Van replied, his tone steeped in a mix of disappointment and resignation. "They cannot fathom that a spiritual being of his magnitude could ever be mistaken about something as crucial as this." In the background, voices clashed. "I'll meet you later, Mendal. I'm setting up base camp; many remain undecided."

Beyond the walls of their home, the clamor of friends and community members in heated conflict swelled. Mendal knew that drastic action was required. The city was fraying at the seams, and he was watching as the force of Lucifer's power threatened to snatch Fay away from him, just as he had been ominously warned.

Perhaps, if he would reveal the visions from the quantum proba-bility computer to her, she might come to see the stark reality. With a heavy resolve, he finally spoke, "Fay, I saw something on a quantum probability computer."

"What did you see?" she asked, her curiosity mingled with a flicker of hope.

Before he could begin, a sudden, commanding voice erupted within his consciousness: *No! Don't tell her!* The shout reverberated through his mind, and he gasped, recoiling as if a powerful, unseen hand had forcefully shoved him back.

"What's wrong with you, Mendal?" Fay asked with genuine con-cern. "What did you see?" she pressed.

"Nothing," he finally replied. And with that final note of resigna-tion, the unsaid truths and unresolved mysteries hung heavy in the silence between them.

CHAPTER 21

Weeks later, Mendal met Zee behind his house away from the chaotic nightmare that had overtaken the city. He craved a quiet moment to speak without the urban despair. Together, they ambled through a sprawling grassy meadow toward the rugged foothills.

"Zee, I hope you can advise me," Mendal began. He hesitated for a moment, a stark contrast to the unwavering authority expected of a leader who must know all the answers. Zee offered a reassuring nod, his expression calm.

"First, where did you come from?" Mendal inquired, his eyes gleaming with an almost desperate longing for clarity. "Before you became one with us on Earth, what were you? What form did you take?"

With a serene cadence, Zee replied, "Before I came to Earth, I existed as pure energy. I was present, though not in the tangible, personified way you now perceive me."

They continued their journey until Mendal found solace under the cool shade of a massive oak tree. Resting against the rough bark, he turned to Zee and asked, "Where did you exist, Zee?"

"In frequency energy circuits," Zee explained. "It was like being inside one of your system broadcasters or radios. I had the ability to tune the bands to endless frequencies, each one unfolding a pathway to a distinct corner of the universe."

Mendal nodded thoughtfully. "Yes, I understand the concept of frequency energy circuits. I haven't ventured into them myself, but my studies have revealed much of their mystery."

With a hint of frustration, Zee added, "Even now in a personality form, I can journey freely, tuning in and out of these frequencies to reach any location in the universe. That was before the system circuits were deactivated."

After a reflective pause, Mendal continued, "Do you still have access to those frequencies?"

"I can leave this life-functioning realm and travel to others," Zee acknowledged, "but only in a limited capacity. The quarantine keeps relentlessly pulling me back to Earth."

They walked in silence for a half mile until Mendal resumed the conversation. "Can humans enter the frequency energy circuits?" he asked. "I know the angelic realms have that ability, yet is it also true for us in physical form?"

"It is indeed possible for humans to enter these circuits from Earth," Zee replied. "However, it requires a profound scrambling of your psychic channels, a delicate disruption of your natural state."

Abruptly, Zee halted and stood perfectly still, his eyes closing as he slipped into a deep meditative state to probe the mysteries of the subject. Moments later, his eyes opened with sudden intensity. "There exists a certain chemical that can allow the human psyche to free fall into various alternate frequencies," he revealed. "Yet, it is extraordinarily difficult to control or predict the journey of an untrained traveler through these shifting bands."

As the duo resumed their trek, Zee cautioned, "These frequencies serve every species in the universe, they are the pathways to other time-realities and dimensions. Remember, Mendal, not all time-realities harbor friendly inhabitants. The gift of free will has allowed truly evil beings to nest in some places. I advise never to venture onto the frequency highway without a prober roadmap."

Eventually, as their path led them from the open expanse of the meadow into a dense, shadowy wooded area, Mendal's frustration bubbled over. Running his hands through his hair, he spun around to face Zee. "Zee, I'm entangled in a dilemma that seems utterly insoluble."

"How can I help?" Zee inquired.

"The problem is that I can't share this secret with anyone as it revolves around probabilities," Mendal confessed.

Zee nodded in understanding. "If people were to know, the very probabilities would shift."

"Yes, I saw something I wasn't meant to see," Mendal admitted, his confession tumbling out in desperation. "You mean too much to me, Zee. I need you to understand why I've delayed my decision."

"I trust you, Mendal," Zee responded with sincere warmth. "Do not risk revealing any more details. Allow me to see if I might uncover any clues." Closing his eyes, he concentrated deeply, his entire focus channeled into the unraveling of hidden threads.

Several minutes passed in profound silence before his head jerked upward in alarm and he gasped, his eyes wide with terror. "Your future is in danger. Extreme danger," he warned.

"Danger from what, Zee?" Mendal asked, his voice trembling as he tried to interpret the unnerving look that had overtaken his companion. A cold shudder ran deep within him.

Zee's expression grew grave as he explained, "Someone or something blocked me from fully seeing. I promise, though, to keep a watch over you, Mendal." Leaning in as if to share a solemn secret, he added, "But do not let anyone learn of what you saw."

With that final, resonant warning, Zee vanished, leaving Mendal beneath the trees, overwhelmed by the weight of Zee's newfound threat.

CHAPTER 22

A sharp, insistent rap on the door jolted Mendal from a light sleep. He groggily lifted his head from the narrow, uncomfortable cot and squinted out the window. The sky was still painted in the muted hues of pre-dawn. "Barely sunrise", he muttered under his breath, a hint of irritation tinging his voice. "Who wants me this early?"

The rap came again, more forceful this time. Mendal stumbled his way to the door, his movements sluggish and unsteady. With a swift jerk, he flung it open, eyes blazing with a touch of madness. "What do you want!" he bellowed, his voice echoing in the stillness of the morning.

Standing before him was an imposing, towering figure, its entire form encased in a metallic shell that gleamed ominously under the early morning light. The only exception to this armored exterior was a horrifying face, a grotesque blend of human and machine—flesh seamlessly melded with mechanical components. The morning sun glinted off an intricate design etched into the metal on its chest, a majestic gold dragon, its body coiling elegantly, scales detailed with such precision that they seemed to ripple with life.

"Caligastia wants you at his office immediately," the courier announced, his voice emerging in a mechanical tone.

"Why?" Mendal demanded, suspicion lacing his words.

"I was instructed to summon you to his office, sir," the courier replied with mechanical precision. "I am to wait and escort you over."

"Well, don't worry about it. I'll be there when I get ready," Mendal snapped, his words sharp as he slammed the door shut.

Standing alone, his face ashen with dark shadows under his eyes, Mendal allowed a wave of emptiness, a dull, gnawing ache in his soul, to overtake him. He bowed his head and shook it, whispering into the silence, "Fay, are you up?" When no answer came, his worry grew as he called again, "Fay?"

At that moment, the bedroom door creaked open and Fay emerged, fully dressed, a suitcase in her grasp and sorrowful determination in her eyes. "I'm leaving, Mendal. I made my feelings known last night and so did you," her voice trembling with resignation.

"Where will you stay?" Mendal inquired. In that moment, he was determined, almost desperately, to prove to Fay and to himself that her departure would not shatter him. After all, he was in charge of operations in Dalamatia. He had enough to worry about without her causing problems.

Fay's eyes flickered with a mix of sadness and defiance. "I'm going to—I'm sure you'll find out soon enough," she said, the words hanging in the air before she blurted out, "You won't listen to my friends or even make an effort to see my point of view."

"I know your views, Fay," Mendal said emotionlessly. The time for argumentation had passed. Clearly, she was no longer either willing or capable of listening to reason.

Tears now streaming down her face, Fay pleaded, "Why do you insist on living in Dalamatia if you won't commit to Lucifer?" she sobbed. "Why don't you just go and live with Van and the others at Michael's camp?" Her voice implored him to see things her way, but she was not so naive as to think that he would.

"Because I haven't decided yet," Mendal replied, his voice weighed down by secrets. "There is a reason, Fay. I just can't tell you what it is." With every fiber of his being, he wanted to just say it. But he could not. The price was too high. The stakes too dire.

"I'm leaving, Mendal," she declared once more and as her voice broke so did the dam of her tears. She opened the door and stepped out, pausing momentarily before slowly turning back, her eyes pleading. "I love you, Mendal, but you're not devoted to Lucifer, and I am."

Without a second glance, she hurried down the steps and made her way to four friends waiting anxiously at the edge of the street.

Mendal followed, descending the stairs with heavy steps. Wrath and tears fought for control of his emotions as he watched her depart. *Damn you, Lucifer,* he thought, outraged. *You took another away from me.* A chill, as penetrating as the cold steel of a knife, pierced his heart. "Okay, I'm ready," he said to the metallic figure in a cool, icy tone.

CHAPTER 23

Mendal strode into the administrative headquarters, the polished marble floors echoing beneath his boots. He was ushered at once into Caligastia's private office, a high-ceilinged chamber lit by a pair of brass sconces that cast long shadows over dark wood paneling. "Nobody's here," he muttered, his voice tight, as he approached a vast mahogany table gleaming under a single overhead lamp. The silence felt ominous.

Was this some sort of trick? He needed to calm down and get control of himself. There was no way he was going to show any sign of weakness to Caligastia. He lifted a crystal tumbler from the table's edge and filled it with water from a silver pitcher. He set the glass down and waited, his every nerve on edge.

Fifteen minutes later, Caligastia entered with Hammone and an aide. Caligastia's cloak brushed the floor; his bearing was regal, unhurried. Talking on a communicator, he gave coordinates and brief instructions to the aide. The aide took notes before slipping out a side door.

"Apologies for the delay, Mendal," Caligastia said. "It's been rather … chaotic." His communicator let out a soft triple beep. Raising it to his ear, Caligastia's expression went distant; he spoke in muted tones, then turned to Hammone. "Lucifer said, 'Do it.'" Hammone nodded, then departed like a shadow.

"Well, that's it," Caligastia said with a sigh of relief. "Mendal, I'm not one to mince words. I just initiated an attack against Michael's loyalists."

Mendal's eyes went wide; his jaw clenched until his teeth ground together. His heart thundered in his chest. Attack Michael's loyalists? All of his worst suspicions had now been confirmed. He stared at Caligastia, fury coiling inside him, yet no protest escaped his lips.

Caligastia measured the "go-to-hell" tilt of Mendal's chin. "Lucifer has pressed for this strike for weeks," he said, turning his back to Mendal. "He and I agree, they must be punished for refusing to side with him. Until now, we've done nothing."

"Why wasn't I notified about this plan earlier?" Mendal asked bluntly, barely keeping his composure. "I am third in command here."

"Lucifer is not sure whether your loyalty is to him or Michael," Caligastia answered, still not facing Mendal. "There is no time limit on your decision, but your hesitation has greatly concerned him. It seems many are waiting on you, Mendal."

"I refuse to discuss this, Caligastia," said Mendal, his voice rising perceptibly in volume. "This is my decision and I will not be rushed."

Caligastia spun around and looked Mendal squarely in the face. "As of now, you are out of the command loop. You will keep your title and responsibilities running day-to-day operations here on Earth, but all upper-level communications, decisions and strategies will be handled only by myself and Hammone."

Mendal's muscles rippled; he seized Caligastia by the shoulders, nails biting into cloth. "How long has Lucifer been able to breach the quarantine? From the very start?"

"Yes, Mendal, from day one," Caligastia said with a contemptuous laugh, jerking away from Mendal's grasp. "You're just a pawn in his plans. The sooner you realize this and acknowledge Lucifer's rightful place as ruler of Radania, the better chance you have of surviving this ordeal."

Fists clenched tightly at his sides, Mendal felt a raw, primal urge surging through him, a burning desire to tear Caligastia apart. His muscles tensed as he fought to contain the explosive force within, the kind of rage that demanded immediate and ferocious action.

Caligastia, feeling Mendal's anger, waved him away with a dismissive gesture and pressed his communicator to his ear. Mendal raised his arm, knuckles white, ready to strike . . . then restraint. Not here, not yet. He had to warn Van. Now!

He stormed from the chamber, boots pounding the corridor. Hammone slipped in through the side door. As soon as he reached the streets, Mendal stood perfectly still and entered a meditative state. *Zee, I know you can hear me. Warn Van. An attack by Caligastia against the loyalists is imminent. Warn them, Zee. Don't let them be slaughtered!*

Caligastia, watching Mendal from his office window, turned to Hammone. "This is just too damned easy."

CHAPTER 24

Seventy-five dedicated staff members and their Andonite assistants joined Van in constructing their new encampment at the rugged foothills northeast of the city. A two-hundred-foot wall of jagged rock provided a formidable defensive barrier for Michael's loyalists. This solid barricade offered much-needed protection against two potentially lethal adversaries: the fierce tribespeople to the south and Caligastia's menacing troops in the city to the southwest.

Around the clock, vigilant guards maintained a watchful eye, successfully holding Caligastia's forces at bay, while delicate peace negotiations kept the tribespeople from launching an attack. The loyalists found shelter in modest tents, with only a few nestled under the sparse cover of the trees, and in the natural, hollowed-out caves within the rocks.

Although the forest seemed more inviting, its allure was overshadowed by the danger of potential raids from the tribespeople. After six tense months, the ever-present threat of assault or ambush from either side became a constant worry, an anxiety they reluctantly adapted to live with.

***

Hammone, accompanied by three stern-faced soldiers, tapped his foot with mounting impatience. The sluggish, barrel-shaped tribesman eventually noticed them and began to amble in their direction with a leisurely gait.

"I told you to hurry," Hammone shouted, his voice slicing through the air and prompting the stocky informer to lumber toward them with a newfound urgency. "We've been waiting nearly an hour!"

"Yes, sir," the tribesman muttered breathlessly, his eyes widening in alarm like a startled deer. "Had to get men, like you wanted."

"How many did you get?" Hammone demanded, his tone laced with skepticism.

"Lots of them," the informer replied, his lips moving silently as he counted on his fingers. "I got lots, maybe twenty!"

Hammone rolled his eyes. "We need more than that!" he said, shaking his head in disgust, his voice dripping with disdain. "We need lots more—what's your name again?"

"Knef," the tribesman blurted out, his voice barely above a whisper. "Knef, sir."

"Well, Knef," Hammone growled, his voice low and threatening, "we'll need more than that. What did you promise them?"

"Like you say," Knef stammered, his words tumbling out in a rush. "They attack and fight, they become gods, like you." He managed a weak grin. "See, I remembered what to say."

"Yes, Knef real smart," Hammone mocked, his sarcasm eliciting snickers from the soldiers. "There's a hundred of you working in the city," Hammone continued, jabbing a finger into Knef's chest with forceful emphasis, "so I expect thirty more to volunteer for duty tomorrow morning before sunrise."

"Yes . . . thirty more," Knef mumbled, nodding with resigned acceptance.

"Or I'll hang you as a traitor," Hammone threatened, his words as cold as ice, "in front of all your friends and family."

"No! Knef don't want to die!" he exclaimed, recoiling in horror, his face a mask of dread as he stumbled back a few steps.

"Then, do it!" Knef turned and waddled down the street, calling out with frantic urgency, waving his arms and shouting, "Need volunteers!" to all who crossed his path.

A soldier shook his head, his expression one of disdain and disgust. "That's all they're good for," he said caustically, his words dripping with contempt. "Good for a slaughter."

***

Fifty tribespeople gathered at the city gates before sunrise, hearts pounding with feverish devotion. Each one desperate to prove his worth, to seize a spark of divinity. Knef stood among them, chest swelling with the pride of a hero.

Before the crowd, Hammone swaggered, hands clasped behind his back. "They won't see you coming," he lied in a cold, measured tone. "They'll be sleeping curled up in tents and caves. Slip past the barrier and slit every throat." A ripple of anxious whispers rose as the massive wooden doors groaned open.

On the other side, the loyalists waited. Behind a wall of rough-hewn boulders piled at the base of the barrier, seventy-five defenders crouched with bows strung, clubs gripped. Van was one of them. None had ever tasted real battle, but their faith in God was ironclad. Their breaths came in ragged puffs of steam as dust swirled around their feet.

Then the earth tremored; a low rumble heralding the first wave of attackers. Muscles coiled, hearts thundered. In a heartbeat Van sprang up and shot the first arrow. It tore into a young tribesman's chest; the man staggered, eyes gone blank, and collapsed into the path of the next.

Twenty arrows hissed from the defenders' bows, ten finding flesh. Another volley, and ten more bodies slumped. Among the dead, Knef's skull split open in a spray of crimson.

The second wave of tribespeople, their attack route to the loyalists littered with dead and dying bodies, gave up the assault and bolted back to the city walls. Despite cries and pleas, the gates were not opened; direct orders from Hammone.

In desperation, the tribespeople clawed at and attempted to climb the walls. Their screams battered the defenders' resolve; yet no soldier stirred to open the gate. Despite Van's plea for mercy, the loyalists reloaded with cold precision and unleashed a final hail of arrows. Every attacker fell silent.

***

The loyalists rejoiced in a frenzy, drums beating triumph into the afternoon. Van watched their wild dances with revulsion. Vicious beasts, that was what they'd become. And something about the attack felt too easy, too reckless. Why no backup? Why risk an attack with no contingency plan?

Drawn by unease, Van slipped beyond the walls and plunged into the forest. An hour of haunted wandering brought him to the crackle of conflict. He hid under brush and fallen trees.

Peering through the branches, he saw squads of city troops patrolling, stun guns humming and clubs poised. They rounded up tribespeople by the dozens, manhandling them into crude wooden cages. Anyone who struggled was beaten until broken.

Van was petrified with shock and disgust. Never had he seen such a gruesome sight. Those who witnessed quickly surrendered. They preferred being caged to being killed. Other screaming tribespeople valiantly fought for their freedom, some savagely beaten and left for dead as examples.

The city troops were on a slave hunt. Cages on crude wheels lumbered through the forest, hauling dozens of tribespeople to their new homes inside the city walls. Those who resisted too vigorously were simply slain, their butchered bodies thrown aside and left as food for gibbons.

The screams were too much for Van to stomach. He became violently ill, both his hands covering the retching sound and abhorrent bodily fluid spurting from his mouth. There was nothing he could do to help.

In a flash, it was suddenly clear to Van. The earlier city attack against the loyalists had been a diversion. Caligastia's true intent had been to capture slaves for the city dwellers. Without diversion, the loyalists, while hunting or exploring, would surely have seen and disrupted this slave hunt.

But now, they were too busy celebrating their pseudo-victory against the city to notice the nearby slaughter. Van knew that Caligastia couldn't take the chance that loyalists and tribespeople might band together against him. Word of the massacre would quickly spread throughout the region and guarantee tribal hatred of anyone different from themselves.

Not only had Caligastia succeeded in gaining slaves for the city dweller's personal use, he had also guaranteed that loyalists and tribespeople would never be allied against him. Van resolved that day not to tell anyone about Caligastia's scheme. If the loyalists found out they were used as dupes, while innocent tribespeople were being massacred, they might never recover. Their morale would be shattered.

Why won't Mendal make his decision? Van wondered. A moment of reflection brought Van to the unthinkable. *Could it be that Mendal is in league with Lucifer?*

CHAPTER 25

Six long months later, Mendal sat solitary in the middle row of the Planetary Amphitheater. Every flicker of the dim gaslights painted shifting, eerie shadows in dark corners, time-worn crevices and murky recesses of the old crumbling brick structure where unseen spirits lurked with watchful eyes.

The heavy door of the theater swung wide with a creak. Van entered, each step labored, and his features etched with weariness. Once filled with boundless energy, he now appeared defeated and drained by relentless battles against the dark forces that had invaded his city, his planet, even his entire galaxy.

Barely a moment later, Fay glided in. Her striking beauty was marred by a pain that resided deep within her heart, a wariness born both of physical exhaustion and emotional upheaval. To her, Michael embodied a brand of evil as undeniable as Lucifer was to Van.

An intense tension charged the air as Van deliberately distanced himself from Fay, their mutual disdain radiating an aura of imminent conflict. With deliberate steps, Van ascended the worn stands and took a seat beside Mendal.

"The angels have confirmed the news," he declared with somber urgency, "Michael has chosen Earth to be His bestowal planet. And now, planets across the galaxy are waiting for Earth to decide before they pledge allegiance to Michael or Lucifer."

Mendal's silent nod conveyed a deep understanding as the weight of destiny pressed upon him.

Van continued, his tone steeped in desperation. "The numbers stand evenly: one hundred and one souls pledged to Michael, one hundred and one loyal to Lucifer. Your decision, Mendal, will now determine the fate of Earth and the entire Radania system."

He draped his arm around Mendal's shoulders, his voice lowering to a haunting whisper. "I have an uneasy feeling that delay will force fate's hand and something drastic will occur." With those words, Van and Mendal descended the stands. Mendal walked a few steps to distance himself from Van and the destiny he refused to acknowledge.

Just then, Fay's presence broke the tension as she advanced toward Mendal. "There is no Father in Paradise, Mendal," she challenged, her words laced with self-righteous fervor. "Michael of Nebadon crafted His own legend to comfort the weak. The truth is that personal liberty grants Lucifer the right to command anyone at will, because only the strong truly prevail. On Earth, as throughout the universe, survival belongs to the fittest, and I stand with them."

Fay pressed her influence, attempting to weave a seductive and dangerous spell upon Mendal's already burdened soul. "Those born with advantages in intelligence and racial purity bear the duty to cleanse Earth and the entire universe of the undesirable misfits of nature," she said, a faint, sinister smile curling on her lips as she tenderly stroked Mendal's face with both of her soft, cool hands.

The theater door groaned open once more. All eyes snapped to Caligastia, who strode into the arena with calm authority. In a swift, graceful motion, Fay fell into line beside him, her arm draped around his waist as if drawn by an irresistible force.

With a measured gesture, Caligastia gently eased Fay aside. Approaching Mendal with the reassuring intimacy of a brother, he wrapped an arm firmly around his shoulders. "Lucifer has given me his assurance," Caligastia said in a low, persuasive tone, "that if you can cast aside this myth of a hidden Father in a fabricated Paradise, he will crown you as the planetary god of your own chosen sphere. Imagine, Mendal, any planet you desire could be yours."

He paused, allowing the tantalizing promise of power and prestige to embed itself in Mendal's thoughts before resuming his relentless mental siege. "But be warned, Mendal, Lucifer values your decision above all and will not hesitate to destroy you if—"

"Do not threaten me, Caligastia," Mendal interrupted, stepping back with his face draining of color, his fists clenching tight and his voice trembling with determination. "I have not yet made up my mind. I need time to weigh both sides before I commit. I refuse to be forced into a decision until I am truly ready!"

Suddenly, the building convulsed with a deafening roar of thunder. The ground trembled and the ancient walls shuddered as if in protest. Then, as if a mystical hush had fallen over the amphitheater, time itself seemed to momentarily shift, transporting the space to some unknown realm.

"There is no more time, Mendal. Choose now! Embrace the radiant life of a planetary god!"

Mendal's voice quivered in defiance. "No, I have not decided yet! I will not be forced into a choice until I am ready!"

"Do it, Mendal! Make your decision! NOW!" The demand rang out, echoing against the stone like a fatal verdict.

"Please, I need more time. Give me more time!" he pleaded desperately.

In that jaw-dropping instant, a searing bolt of electricity ripped through Mendal's body with such ferocity that the brightness seared into the eyes of everyone present, leaving them temporarily blinded.

As vision gradually returned, Fay's eyes frantically scanned the scene, her mind reeling in disbelief and shock. "He's gone!" she cried out, her voice choked with a mix of astonishment and fear. "Mendal's gone!"

Chapter 26

The principal, engrossed in files spread across his polished desk, raised his eyes slowly as Mendal stepped into the room. This room was no stranger to Mendal, it was precisely the same one he had visited on two previous occasions, its every detail unchanged. Mendal felt as though he had just slipped out mere moments ago, only to be drawn back into a space steeped in familiarity and quiet authority.

"Be seated," the principal commanded, his tone edged with irritation. "I'll explain the reason you were summoned here."

Mendal's eyes darted around the room, absorbing every unchanged line and shadow. For an instant, a whisper urged him to flee, but that thought withered under the weight of reality. Lowering himself into the chair with heavy reluctance, he let his head droop, shoulders surrender into a slumped posture and his hands bury themselves in his face.

The principal's gaze moved deliberately over his collection of papers, the silence punctuated by the rustle of turning pages. "You have been summoned here by the Most Highs," he pronounced. At that moment, brilliant light streamed through an opening in the ceiling directly above, washing the chamber in a glow that seemed to whisper of divine judgment.

"The Lucifer rebellion," the principal continued, "is now spiraling beyond control, threatening to engulf other systems." As if in response, the golden radiance intensified, deepening in hue and pulsing with a newfound vitality. "Had the previous personality you assumed on Earth possessed the resolve to decide as fate intended, this rebellion would already be consigned to history."

A note of desperation colored Mendal's voice as he attempted to craft his own narrative of innocence. "Why don't the Ancients of Days simply annihilate the rebels?" he inquired. "Is it because they truly lack the power to stop Lucifer?"

"There exist forty-eight reasons why evil is allowed to run its full course," the principal replied in a tone as cold and unyielding as the stone walls surrounding them. A dismissive turn of his head was an unmistakable gesture of disdain.

Facing the stark truth in the principal's silence, Mendal's hopes of receiving a comforting explanation began to crumble. With a heavy sigh of resignation, he tilted his gaze upward toward the celestial light.

Is it my destiny to become as a planetary god, as Lucifer claims? Or am I merely destined to be swept into the extinction of spiritual existence?

In the quiet aftermath of his query, no answer, no divine consolation, no guiding sign came forth, only the oppressive silence of unanswered fate. Steadying himself with a deep, measured breath, Mendal wrestled with the need to share what he had witnessed on the quantum probability computer. *Surely,* he thought, *the principal would finally understand.* "There's a reason I haven't yet announced a decision! I saw—" he began, his voice trembling with urgency.

Abruptly, the principal pivoted in his chair at an unsettling speed. "Do you have something to confess, Mendal?" he inquired before Mendal could complete his thought. A heavy silence ensued before the principal lifted his gaze once more toward the heavens. "It has been decreed that you be placed in a neutral environment and granted all the time necessary to reach your decision."

Mendal's mind raced as he processed the weight of these words. Suddenly, his eyes flashed open wide with dawning comprehension, and he sprang to his feet in alarm. "What do you mean by 'placed in a neutral environment'? You can't possibly mean—" he stammered.

Before he could finish, the golden light from above surged downward, its radiant beams encasing Mendal, as though sealing his fate.

***

The blinding lights of a bustling hospital delivery room illuminated a nurse cradling a newborn infant tenderly in her arms. The doctor, his smile warm and assured, leaned down to address the young mother. "Congratulations, Mrs. Brueggemann," he announced proudly, "It's a boy!"

CHAPTER 27

A shrill, insistent signal broke the silence of the chamber, alerting Lucifer to the arrival of an anticipated visitor. Lean and statuesque, his frame draped in finely tailored slacks and a snug sweater, he slowly straightened his posture and rose gracefully from behind his imposing black glass desk. Meanwhile, a relentless flurry of keystrokes continued, as ghostly images and rapidly shifting pictures danced and blurred across a vast monitor.

The luxurious room was encircled by video screens, each projecting live feeds from different sectors of the Radania galaxy, their vibrant hues contrasting with the black velvet draping the walls, elegantly accented by gleaming gold.

Lucifer made his way to the south wall where an elevator door awaited him. With silent precision, he mentally disengaged the security mechanism. Before his eyes, an elderly servant with a voice weathered by time and burden stepped forward from the elevator. "Sir, a message from Caligastia," he announced in a cracked tone. Stepping out into the charged atmosphere, the servant paused, waiting for further instructions.

Lucifer's eyes flared a deep, sinister crimson as he tilted his head downward, fixating his gaze on the floor below as if seeking hidden truths in the very ground. "I can discern three probabilities attached to this message," he growled. "Probability number one: Mendal has made his decision, and that decision has gained him godship over a planet of his choosing. Yet, I have never sanctioned such an elevation, so that possibility must be ruled out."

His measured tone carried a blend of disdain and calculated precision. "Probability number two: Mendal's choice has somehow precipitated a rebellion against me. But here I stand, unbroken and unbound by any prison world or tribunal, which dismisses that eventuality as well. That leaves us with probability number three."

At those charged words, Lucifer's body underwent a breathtaking metamorphosis. The dormant Rage within him was roused, surging forth like molten fire, imbuing him with a vibrant, dangerous glow.

His skin seared as if touched by blistering heat and his garments disintegrated into nothingness under the overwhelming energy. This transformation was nothing short of titanic. The slender, refined figure expanded monstrously, fueled by the pure savagery, decadence and wrath of Rage, until his once modest form now loomed ten times his former size, an imposing colossus imbued with raw menace.

"They interfered!" roared the unbridled spirit of Rage. "They took Mendal away! That was never part of our agreement!" In a frenzied outburst of uncontrolled power, even as the servant's desperate, guttural pleas for mercy filled the room, Rage's massive fist descended with devastating force, crushing the pitiful soul into oblivion.

For nearly an hour, Lucifer's Rage reigned supreme, a storm of uncontrolled fury. Only when the upheaval subsided did Lucifer emerge, stepping out of his Rage-driven form to reclaim the calm, calculating persona that defined him.

Separated as two distinct entities, the subdued, methodical Lucifer resumed his place at the desk. He retrieved a file from a leather briefcase and began inputting critical data into his quantum computer, a silent testament to his unwavering command of both chaos and order.

Meanwhile, Rage lingered in the center of the room, watchful and simmering.

Focused intently on the flickering, cryptic data streaming from the monitor, Lucifer beckoned his servant once more. The servant, the same elderly man Rage had crushed earlier, presented a compact, hand-held communicator with trembling hands. Without hesitation, Lucifer pressed a ruby button on the device and declared, "Satan, be here in one hour."

Rage let out a deep, guttural growl, a primal sound as ancient as the cosmos. His colossal arms rose skyward and the raw seismic power radiating from him made the ground tremble in response. Locking eyes with Lucifer, the two aspects of his being seemed to evaluate the situation in silent communion. "We've got to move on this now!" they voiced simultaneously.

True to the appointed hour, Satan arrived. He nodded respectfully to the serene Lucifer but cautiously kept his distance from the intimidating presence of Rage. He dared not approach or even meet the ferocious glare emanating from the Rage, well aware of his unpredictable and uncontrollable nature.

"You remember my other half," Lucifer remarked to Satan, extending an arm toward the monstrous form of Rage. In response, Rage turned to Satan with a menacing glare. Shielding his face with his left hand, Satan nodded warily. *I don't need the stress of him here, watching everything I do,* Satan thought.

"I'm keeping him around until Mendal visits," Lucifer mused, a sly amusement dancing in his eyes as he observed the tense interplay between Satan and Rage.

Should I leave while there's still a chance? Satan's anger erupted into an unstoppable blaze, his entire being boiling with fear and fury.

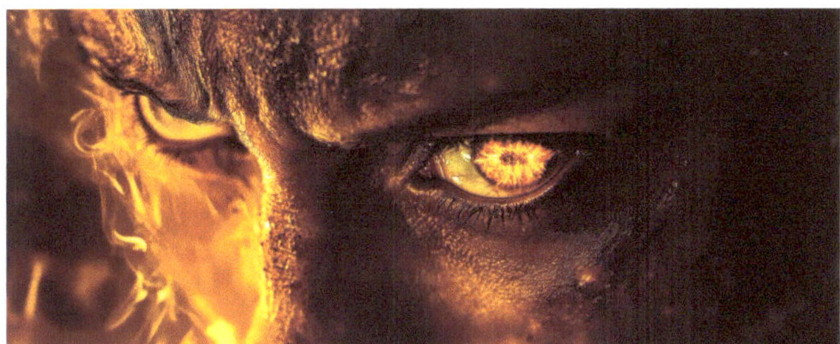

"You're right, Satan, I am watching everything you do," bellowed Rage. "I know every thought that crosses your mind. But don't be anxious or flee, Satan. I won't kill you. At least, I will try to restrain myself!" His booming laughter reverberated through the room.

"Mendal has been dispatched to Earth's twentieth century," Lucifer remarked, his irritation growing, "and he must still make his decision." A cold and calculating smirk crossed his face as he shot a piercing glance in Satan's direction. "Or be destroyed before he can."

Contemplating Lucifer's words, Satan's lips curved into a smile of malicious delight. "I understand exactly what you mean, Lucifer. I will make sure that Fay is waiting for him. He won't be able to resist her."

Lucifer's gaze held an unnerving intensity as he issued his final command. "You, Satan, must be there, too. Get Mendal to declare his decision for me. If you can't do it, if he hesitates or appears leaning toward Michael, make sure he visits me," Lucifer said confidently. "Rage will take care of him."

CHAPTER 28

"Mendal, you are here to make your decision. You will be given every opportunity to choose between the ways of God or the ways of Lucifer. You must decide for yourself whether God exists, or God does not exist."

"Mommmmm!" screamed John, jolting himself awake from the depths of a vivid dream. His heart pounded as he sat up, eyes wide with alarm. "Mom, there are voices in my head! They're calling me Mendal! They want me to be good, not bad! Mom, am I bad? Mommmmm!"

John's mom hurried into the dimly lit room. She sat gently beside him on the bed, her presence a comforting calm amid his storm of confusion. "Of course you're not bad, sweetheart," she assured him as she smoothed his tousled hair. "You're my little angel. You just had a nightmare, that's all. And do you remember what day this is?"

"It's my birthday! I remember, Mom!" John exclaimed, the initial panic in his eyes replaced by an eager sparkle.

"Yes, and how old are you today?" she asked, her smile warm and encouraging.

"I'm six years old! I'm a big boy now, huh Mom!" John declared, his face lighting up with pride.

"Yes, you are," she replied. "And we're going swimming at your favorite pool with all your friends today."

"Is Dad coming with us?" John inquired with a hint of hopefulness.

She recalled hearing him arrive home around three in the morning, the creak of the stairs echoing as he stumbled to bed, still clothed and enveloped in the pervasive scent of cigarettes and beer. She had laid still, feigning sleep as he settled beside her.

"Is he coming?" John asked again, his small voice tinged with anticipation.

"I'm afraid not, dear," she answered with a deep sigh. "He's not feeling well."

"Oh," John responded. He paused thoughtfully, then sat up with newfound determination. "Mom, you know that talk we had about God?"

"Yes, dear," she replied.

"Mom, I think God came inside me last night and talked to me," John said earnestly.

John's mom nodded. "He's inside all of us, sweetheart," she said, her smile reassuring. "God's always with you."

"But you know what Dad said. He said God isn't real. He says there is no God. He says—"

"Now don't you listen to your father when he's been drinking," she interrupted, her tone firm yet loving. "You know he's a good man and loves you dearly. He just doesn't know God the way we do."

"Well, Dad told me I need to grow up and be just like him. He said to—"

"John, stop that chatter," she interjected. "Did you forget what today is already?" "It's my birthday!" John shouted with renewed excitement, leaping out of bed ready to embrace the joys of his special day.

CHAPTER 29

John bolted down the nearly deserted high school hallway, his heart pounding as he raced toward senior math class. The fluorescent lights overhead felt overwhelmingly bright today, their harsh glare mirroring the pounding in his head from the previous night's indulgence in too much beer. It was a reckless decision on a school night that now branded him, in his own mind, a complete shithead.

Just as he swung open the heavy classroom door, the tardy bell clanged. With barely a moment to spare, John slid into one of the only two seats left in the front row, a spot notorious for attracting only the most studious or the last-minute arrivals. His eyes darted around the room, noting the absence of the teacher.

"The front row's where all the nerds and latecomers end up," John whispered to a friend sitting a row behind him.

"Yeah, which one are you?" Steve jibed, his laugh echoing a bit too loudly against the high-ceilinged room. Around them, boisterous chatter filled the morning air, as students awakened by the fresh breeze wafting in from open windows eagerly traded weekend stories and plans.

"Heading to the kegger Saturday night?" Steve asked John after a tap on the shoulder. "I know crowds aren't your thing and you're not into the whole jock scene, but you've got to celebrate the Big Eighteen! We partied hard at mine last month. You remember, right?"

"How could I forget?" John replied with a grimace. "I got completely shit-faced and made a total fool of myself. Or at least, that's what I've heard."

"Well, for once in your life, you can actually get legally drunk," Steve remarked with a sly grin.

"Yeah, that's something I can't pass up," John admitted. "I just wish this damned headache would let up."

"Look at you, not even a legal adult and already you're an alcoholic," Steve teased. "You should hear my brother bitch about the drinking age changing to eighteen this year. Poor guy had to wait three more years before he could go to a bar than I did. It really pisses him off."

"Finally, right?" John said, with a sour laugh. "Teenagers were old enough to be drafted and die in 'Nam, but they couldn't drink a fuckin' beer? Man, the law had to change."

The classroom buzz abruptly softened as the teacher strode in, accompanied by a student trailing behind her. Every pair of eyes in the room shifted focus to the new arrival.

"This is Dean," announced Ms. Healey. "He'll be joining us for the last two weeks of the school year."

As she reached to place an arm around Dean's shoulder, the boy recoiled sharply at her touch, his body stiffening in protest. "Don't touch me, you—" He wisely didn't finish the sentence, noted John.

Dean was imposing and unforgettable: black, taller than most for his age, with an immense '70s Afro and a vibrant tie-dyed shirt that clashed stylishly with his dark sunglasses. His bellbottoms, impossibly wide and flamboyant, seemed to announce his arrival long before he spoke.

Instantly, the room erupted into a babble of whispers and chattering. "Wow, that's the new kid from Chicago," Steve whispered. "He's the coolest dude this backwater town has ever seen."

"Yeah, man, check out those bellbottoms and that Afro! This guy's real funky." John declared with genuine admiration. "Did you see the way he didn't take any shit from Healey there? Man, that's what I call cool."

"And that cane he's got? I heard he's legally blind," Steve added. "Mike's been spreading some weird stories about him."

"Weird? Like what?" John pressed, eager for more details.

Before Steve could elaborate, Ms. Healey's sharp slam of her pointer against the chalkboard silenced the room. "John, why don't you show Dean to his desk? We've got a lot to cover today if you want to pass this class and graduate high school."

Just as John started is rise, Steve leaned in close, whispering in his ear, "I heard he don't see with his eyes, but he's got this vision that can like, see right into your soul."

"What?" John muttered, reluctantly abandoning his seat and straightening his posture to look as cool as possible in front of his classmates. He stepped forward, extending his hand with a casual coolness. "Your desk's right over here next to mine, man."

"I know where it is, you homo," Dean sneered as he shoved John aside, using the tap of his cane to locate his desk. John hurriedly retreated to his own seat.

"Yeah, sit down, you homo!" Jimmy hollered from the back of the room, his remark sparking a chorus of laughter that rippled across the class.

Lounging back in his chair, Dean turned slightly toward John, but before he could launch into another cutting remark, he paused and locked eyes with him. That silent stare lingered well into the lesson, only broken by the teacher's voice. "Do we have a problem here, Dean?" she inquired.

"I think he likes John," Jimmy blurted out, sending another round of laughter echoing through the room.

John felt his face flush a deep shade of red. "No, it's okay. I'm sorry for the interruption," Dean said, his voice softening just enough. "Sometimes I drift into different . . . I'm fine now. Go on."

For John, the next forty-five minutes stretched out like an endless eternity. Finally, the bell rang and everyone scattered out the door. As John trudged down the hall toward his next class, a rhythmic tapping sound echoed behind him. He spun around to come face-to-face with Dean.

"Meet me in the parking lot at four sharp, man. I drive the Mustang, can't miss it. It's where all the chicks hang out," Dean instructed with a low chuckle before vanishing into the throng of students hurrying to their next class.

***

Six hours later, John and Steve found themselves in the school parking lot, the ritual of an afternoon hamburger and Pepsi complete. John glanced at his watch. "Hot day. They say it should be in the mid-90s," Steve commented, a master of the obvious. "Man, I'm so ready for summer this year. Just two more weeks and no more high school."

"Yeah," John replied, in no mood for small talk.

John noticed a cluster of people gathered at the far end of the lot. Moving toward them, he was abruptly halted by Steve's firm grip on his arm. "You're not really going over there, are you? Most of those guys aren't even in high school," Steve warned. "They look like they're in their twenties, man. Trust me, don't get involved, John. There's trouble brewing."

Steve's warning did little to sway John. He made a brief stop at his own car, popped a Black Sabbath cassette into the car's high-powered tape player and cranked up the volume. Taking a deep, steadying breath, he strode casually toward the Mustang.

Dean, seemingly oblivious to John's approach, was busy enjoying a long, contemplative drag from a joint. He passed it to a tall brunette woman standing by his side, her hand gently rubbing his ass.

"John, is that you, man?" Dean asked, exhaling a cloud of smoke that mingled with the fresh afternoon air.

"Yeah, how'd you know it was me?" John replied. "You got that 'rich kid' smell. And that Black Sabbath tape? Come on, man. You got some James Brown?" Dean teased.

"Uhhh . . . not with me," John stammered.

"Ha, not with him. Must have left that tape at home," mocked one of the nearby men, drawing hearty laughs from the group. Even John couldn't help but crack a smile.

Sliding an arm around John's shoulder, Dean steered him away from the rowdy crowd. "I've gotta talk to my man here," he announced, prompting the woman to momentarily follow before Dean waved her off. "In private, babe." With that, she sauntered back toward the car.

Guided by the distinctive tap of his cane, Dean led John toward the chain-link fence that bordered the parking lot. John inquired, "So, what's going on, man?"

"Meet me at my place tonight at nine," Dean replied as he pressed a small book of matches into John's hand. "Here's the address." John tucked them securely into his pocket.

"I've got some people I want you to meet," Dean continued. "If you impress them, I can hook you up as a major pot dealer for your rich friends over on the West Side. We're talking big bucks."

"I'll be there," John vowed. "I won't let you down, man."

CHAPTER 30

John's 1950 Ford coupe bounced erratically over four rusted sets of railroad tracks that split the town into the haves and the have-nots. The sound of Grand Funk Railroad filled the car as John rolled down the window to get a better look at the unfamiliar street signs. It was already nine and the long road ahead reminded him of a night marred by too many pool games and pitchers of beer. *Damn,* he thought, *I should have left earlier.*

The unlit streets slowed his journey to a near crawl. At last, John pulled into the parking lot of an aging apartment complex at the end of the block. Two teens watched him with curious eyes as he maneuvered his car close to a building.

With a determined pace, John entered the building and strode toward the elevator, only to be met with a sign reading "Out of Order." "Shit!" he muttered. He bolted up the stairs and down the hallway until reaching room 412.

He paused before the door to catch his breath and summon the courage to knock, reassuring himself that he was hardly worth robbing, his pockets holding nothing more than a few bucks.

He knocked meekly, hoping no one was home. His mind flirted with the promise of another beer and another round of pool. *Had they heard me? Should I knock again?*

Before John could decide, the door swung open. "John, glad you could make it," announced Dean, wearing large, black-framed sunglasses and faded bell-bottom jeans that lent him an effortlessly cool air. "Did you have any trouble finding us poor folk all the way down here on the South Side?"

"No, man, I've been down here loads of times," John replied too quickly.

Dean chuckled mischievously. "Yeah, yeah, just messin' with ya," he said, leading John into the apartment. The living room, furnished with a scattering of chairs and two couches, was occupied by four men, two black and two white, each casting a curious gaze in John's direction.

A striking young woman stood in the middle of the living room, her presence filling the space with an undeniable allure, exuding an air of sensuality. Her eyes, deep and expressive, locked intently on John, conveying a multitude of unspoken thoughts and emotions.

The men radiated formidable, athletic energy. One black man towered over the rest at six feet six and more than three hundred pounds, his bulk dominating most of one of the couches. "Maybe you've heard of Big Willy, John," Dean said with a casual air. "He's the all-conference lineman from RMC."

John nodded slowly, cautiously approaching the couch with an extended hand in a friendly gesture. Big Willy attempted to rise but aborted halfway, his hand colliding with John's as he sank back into the cushions. "Yeah, but don't worry," Big Willy slurred amid a round of hearty laughter, "the school's got me so loaded down on drugs that I couldn't hurt a honky if I wanted to."

A guy in a red shirt quipped, "What's so important, Dean? I need to get my beauty sleep. I mean sleep with my beauties," drawing more laughter as all eyes converged on Dean. Calmly, Dean extracted a wooden chair from the bedroom for John and sat himself on the floor just a few feet away.

"Okay, John, I have a question for you. Answer it right, and you'll see a lot of us . . . and a lot of her," Dean said with a sly smile as he gestured toward the beautiful woman.

With a flirtatious wink, she confirmed his words. "We'll hook you up with the best pot connections. And I'm talkin' Colombian, man!"

John scanned the room, feeling the weight of every stare. *What do they want from me?* John wondered. *Why did anything I have to say mean this much?*

"John, you were born to be a leader of our revolution," Dean declared, his voice full of conviction. "You were meant for this." Rising, Dean placed a firm hand on John's shoulder. "Close your eyes, John, and look into the future with me." John obeyed.

"Relax," Dean whispered. "I'm about to ask you something and answer truthfully, with the answer you believe." John nodded. "What does the future hold? Will it be a revolution against our repressive government, a chance to build our nation in true freedom? Or will everything simply stay the same?"

Lost in thought, John wrestled with Dean's weighty words. The promise was tantalizing; yet he doubted his ability to see into the future. The inner conflict churned: *Why me?*

Drawing a deep, steadying breath, John knew that this decision was his alone, a choice he could not make on a whim, no matter the allure of status or the fear of missing out.

"C'mon, man, it's decision time," Dean pressed, his cool demeanor laced with barely concealed impatience.

All eyes in the room were fixed on him. Finally, John managed, "Dean, I think a guy like you should lead it, not me. I can't commit to such a big decision without really thinking it through."

Dean's nostrils flared as he snapped, "No more time. Indecision is exactly what the man wants! You're either with us or against us. Delaying this is for wimps and cowards. So, tell me, are you a coward, John?"

There was something disturbingly ruthless and manipulative about Dean, a dark, almost evil streak that sent chills down his spine. At other moments, John felt inexplicably comfortable in his presence.

"Make the decision, John," Dean demanded sharply. "Is it revolution?"

John's throat tightened. He opened his mouth to say "revolution," but halted. This decision was too monumental to be taken lightly. Deep within, he searched for the truth: Was there truly a revolution looming? What did the future promise? Suddenly, with startling clarity, he spoke, "Dean, I don't see a revolution in the near future."

"WHAT?" Dean roared, his eyes flashing dangerously as disbelief warped his features. "I can't believe you'd say that!"

John stayed calm. "I just don't see a revolution coming, Dean," he repeated quietly.

Dean's eyes, hidden behind dark lenses, burned with a hatred that pierced deeper than any visible glare. "So, you're saying that life for us, the workers, the poor, the common folk, will only improve if the rich feel generous? That we're doomed to struggle until the wealthy throw us a bone? There's no hope," he said, his voice dripped with contempt.

"No, Dean, I never said that," John countered, reaching out to place a tentative hand on Dean's shoulder. "I just can't promise a great people's revolution when I don't see one."

"Think about it some more, John," Dean pleaded, shrugging off his touch with cold indifference. "It's not too late to change your mind, think of what it means for us. And for you."

At his signal, the seductive woman drifted gracefully over to John. Her touch was gentle but insistent as she caressed his shoulder and chest, her warm breath whispering in his ear, "Decide for the revolution." Then she got down on her knees directly in front of him.

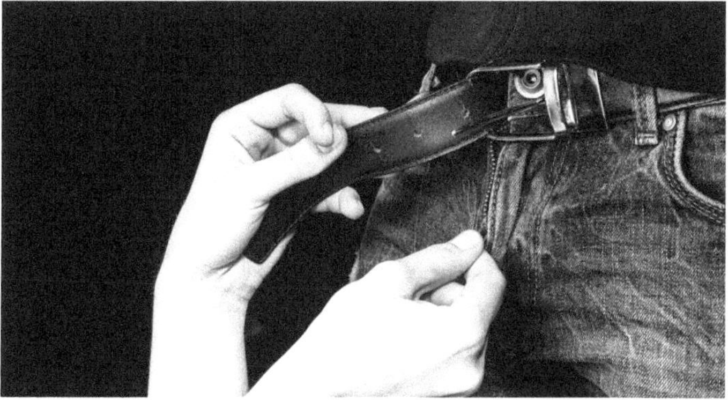

The heat of her body and the suggestive play of her hand on the zipper of his jeans sent a jolt through him, a potent mixture of desire and danger that threatened to overwhelm his resolve. He averted his eyes, trying to refocus his thoughts on the matter at hand.

Abruptly turning back to Dean, John swallowed hard. "I can't make the decision," he insisted. The woman laughed and drifted away.

One by one, Dean's friends shook their heads in disapproval and rose, their eyes darkening with quiet resentment. John felt the peril in the air; it was time to leave. He moved toward the front door, a sense of foreboding accompanying his every step, until suddenly, a firm hand grabbed him and spun him around.

In that terrifying moment, Satan flung his cane against the wall and revealed himself. His eyes burned as he glared at John with unbridled hatred. In a low, venomous tone he hissed, "Go to hell, Mendal. Lucifer's waitin' for 'ya."

CHAPTER 31

John sat with his parents at the dining table for a late evening dinner, the air thick with the aroma of roasted meat and gravy. He absentmindedly pushed the food around his plate, his mind lingering on the keg of beer waiting for him later. The setting sun filtering through the window shades reminded him of the time slipping by.

"Your uncle wants to know if you'll go to church with them on Sunday, John," his mother said with a gentle smile, her eyes hopeful.

"Church! Ha! What a bunch of crap," his father scoffed, wiping a smudge of gravy from his mouth with the back of his hand before taking another hearty swig of his beer.

"Frank, stop that," John's mom admonished. "If John wants to go to church, don't discourage him. Just because you don't believe in God or anything doesn't mean we don't."

John shook his head, a soft chuckle escaping his lips.

"Where are you going tonight, dear?" his mother asked. "Just out," he replied, rising from his seat and making his way toward the door with a casual swagger.

Frank belched loudly, getting up from the table with a groan. "Yeah, probably out to some beer bash or somethin'," he muttered, his voice trailing off as he made his way to the well-worn lounge chair in the living room, beer bottle still clutched in his hand.

You got that right, John thought to himself with a wry grin.

Frank stumbled slightly as he reached for the remote. "Just 'cause you're eighteen doesn't mean you can get drunk every night," Frank hollered.

John stifled a laugh, knowing the remote wasn't where it's supposed to be.

"Where's the remote? It's not on top of the TV Guide where it's supposed to be!" Frank barked.

John grabbed his jacket from the hall closet, feeling the comforting weight of a newly bought bag of pot in its pocket.

"Goddammit, you live here, you follow my rules—" Slam!

***

The cool night air embraced him as he strode purposefully toward the kegger, the promise of the night ahead urging him onward.

A hundred vibrant, young people gathered in an open field bordered by towering pine trees. In the center of it all, a huge bonfire crackled. Overhead, the full moon peeked shyly from behind a slow-drifting cloud, as if acknowledging that the night had officially begun.

John breezed through the crowd. He sipped on frosty beer and exchanged hearty laughs with school friends, gradually melting away his habitual shyness with each passing drink. The music, the chatter and the collective energy of the crowd eased him into a state of excitement. Tonight felt electric, promising memories that would last a lifetime.

Amid the revelry, his gaze landed on a striking girl with flowing light brown hair, a face he recognized from English class. He was almost certain her name was Leslie. Her ensemble was an expression of free-spirited style: ragged, well-worn jeans paired with a loose, revealing hippy blouse accented by layered necklaces and beads. Drawing a deep, steadying breath, John made his way toward her. "Hi, Leslie. I didn't know you went to these things," he said.

Leslie's eyes sparkled with mild surprise. "Oh, hi John. Yeah, well, I didn't know you did, either." Her tone was playful as she reached out to gently caress one of the tassels dangling from the fringed, brown leather jacket he wore. "I like your jacket, John. It's real hip," she said, her smile warm and inviting.

"I like your blouse, too. It really shows you off." Realizing the clumsy phrasing, he quickly corrected himself. "Uh . . . I mean, it looks good on you." The flush on his face deepened as he hoped his awkwardness wasn't too apparent.

Leslie simply laughed. "I know what you mean. Thanks."

Feeling a renewed sense of ease, John leaned forward with a spark of impulsiveness. "Hey, do you want to go get a beer with me?"

"Far out," she replied with an enthusiastic nod.

"Then maybe we can go and smoke a joint, if you want. I've got some really good bud," he added.

Leslie's eyes lit up with mischievous anticipation as she replied, "Sure. I never turn down a doobie." With a shared grin, they both grabbed a cold beer from the keg, then migrated to a secluded, wooded area at the edge of the party.

Leaning casually against the rough bark of a sturdy tree, John skillfully rolled a joint. With a ceremonious inhale, he took a deep draw before passing it over to Leslie, who reciprocated with an enthusiastic drag and a radiant smile as she handed it back.

"Man, this is one of the better keggers of the year," Leslie remarked, "not too wild." After a moment of reflective pause, she added, "I'm really glad I bumped into you, John." Gently, she ran her fingers through his disheveled long hair.

"Yeah, me too," John replied as he clasped her shoulders and captured her lips in a tender kiss. They eased down onto the cool grass, leaning back against the supportive embrace of the tree. As Leslie's kisses grew more fervent, John's responses turned fleeting and subdued, his enthusiasm waning as if distracted.

Noticing the change, a trace of sadness crept into Leslie's expression. Her brow furrowed in concern as she softly queried, "Is it something I did?"

John remained silent, his gaze drifting away for a moment. "John?" she pressed gently. "Are you really that spaced out from just one joint and a few beers?"

After a long pause, John offered a small, distant smile. "I know this sounds kinda weird," he began cautiously, "but I'm planning to go hiking in the mountains by myself tomorrow. I've made a decision, a decision to believe in God and I need to make it official . . . or something like that. I can't explain it fully, but it feels as if some spirits have been waiting for me to decide."

Leslie's interest peaked, her voice filled with wonder. "That's awesome! Really cool. Can I come with you?"

At that sudden intimacy of the moment, John paused, the gravity of his own words sinking in. "Wow, I must be really stoned to be telling you all this tonight," he admitted with a slightly embarrassed chuckle.

Leslie's smile remained gentle and understanding. "It's okay. For some reason, I feel like we've known each other for ages, like in another lifetime." Her hand traveled slowly across his cheek. "Do you know what I mean, John?"

Looking deeply into the midnight blue of her eyes, John replied in a hushed tone, "Yeah, I thought it was just me being stoned, but I just know we've been together before." His mind reached out, grasping at the shadows of memories that were both tantalizingly familiar and frustratingly elusive.

"Not just together, John, but really together." Leslie pressed closer, her gaze intense and filled with passion. "It's as if we created something extraordinary, something born of pure love."

"Yeah, Les," John said softly, "It's like that feeling or memory is there, but . . . I just can't quite remember it."

In an embrace charged with both passion and poignant mystery, Leslie drew John into a deep, soulful kiss. Time seemed to slow as he gently eased her down onto the lush grass. Moments later they both reluctantly pulled apart as the intensity of their passion began attracting curious glances.

"You know Dean, that cool hippie guy from school?" Leslie asked.

"Yeah," John replied, a hint of concern in his eyes as he wondered if Dean had mentioned anything about the previous night.

"He gave me some acid today," Leslie confided, lowering her voice, "but I'm too scared to try it. He said it was pure LSD. I heard it can cause some kind of religious experience sometimes."

John's face relaxed in relief, the tension easing from his features. "Oh," he said quietly.

"I brought it with me, just in case I got the nerve to try," she continued, her eyes twinkling with both mischief and curiosity. "Why don't you take it? You might end up chatting with those spirits or something."

John looked at her curiously. *What could it hurt? Drugs have never been a problem for me before.* She took the acid out of her pocket and gave it to him. He popped it in his mouth. "I'll say 'hi' to God for you, Les."

CHAPTER 32

L ying in the sunbaked grass behind a gnarled oak tree, John began to glimpse bands of electricity crackling in the air. They grew stronger and stronger until his line of vision consisted entirely of these electrical bands. The physical reality he previously was in, the reality of time and substance, slowly dissolved into nothingness before him.

John looked at what he perceived to be a three-dimensional movie screen. But no movie was playing. One single crackling band of electricity rolled up on the screen, paused, then rolled off. Another almost immediately took its place. As these electrical frequencies rolled by, he heard voices talking when the bands stopped, sometimes numerous conversations at once, similar to tuning through radio stations.

In one sudden, blinding flash, a surge of energy tore through layers of memories and psychic residue; every recollection of his former life as Mendal was crystal clear. He was Mendal and he now knew that he always would be Mendal.

Mendal turned his attention to the electrical frequency bands that rolled in front of him. When a band stopped, he tuned into and visualized himself inside that frequency. Not wanting to be drawn in completely, he scanned through the layers of vibrations within the frequency with caution.

To his amazement, each vibration seemed to be a world in that frequency's sector of the universe. However, he didn't know what sector of the universe he was looking at or which world was assigned to a particular vibration. He didn't have the roadmap to the system network. This was what Zee had described. Mendal was in the frequency energy circuits!

Mendal exited the frequency and watched others roll by. Suddenly, the rolling stopped. An ominous, deep hum vibrated around him as one solitary electrical band ignited with an intensity that commanded his attention—and this band refused to move on.

Mendal tuned into the frequency and visualized himself inside. He was drawn toward a familiar vibration. Was it Earth's? He felt a strong spiritual presence all around him.

A voice boomed from the world inside the vibration. "Mendal, Caligastia is after you. He wants you killed before you can formally announce your alliance with God. You are the last one. The proceedings can be delayed indefinitely if you're destroyed before—"

The declaration was abruptly cut short as Mendal was violently ripped from the frequency. The band was replaced by a new, harsher one whose jagged edges crackled with demonic intent. It began to split apart as if someone, or something, were wrenching it open from inside, the separation accompanied by the frightening sound of stretching and tearing.

From the gaping rupture emerged Caligastia, seething with disdain. With nowhere to hide, Mendal faced the full fury of his tormentor. "This will send you to hell, you bastard, where Lucifer will annihilate you!" Caligastia smacked Mendal, hitting him with the fury of his rage. Mendal was knocked almost entirely out of his mind by the blow.

Overwhelmed by a harrowing sensation of endless descent, Mendal felt as if he were being hurled headlong into a vast, unfathomable abyss. He plunged through layers of a planet's atmosphere, the raw, icy wind whipping past his skin. He fell for what seemed like an eternity, terrified, uncertain and without hope of reprieve, until, finally, darkness claimed his consciousness.

When Mendal awoke, his eyes widened in horror at the desolate wasteland that stretched infinitely around him, a world stripped bare of life and hope. Twin suns blazed overhead, radiating an unbearable, flesh-searing heat upon the barren landscape of blistering red dirt and rugged rock hills.

His battered face was pressed into the coarse dirt as Mendal attempted to rise, but an invisible force pressed him downward, like fiery hands relentlessly clawing, burning and digging into his flesh. The pressure increased, pushing him deeper and deeper through successive layers of searing, red-hot clay until he crashed into an underground cavern. The cavern's walls glowed dimly with an eerie, dark-amber light, radiating unbearable heat and an odor so potent and putrid it seared his nostrils.

Motionless and trapped in a waking nightmare, Mendal lay there expecting the torment to be mere illusion, only to soon realize that no ordinary nightmare could inflict such excruciating pain and deep-rooted fear. Summoning all his strength, he slowly attempted to rise, each movement a battle against unyielding agony, his vision blurred and his body trembling uncontrollably. Collapsing into a heap, he tried to cry out in anguish, only to find his voice stolen away by the oppressive force.

As his sight began to clear bit by bit, he scanned the cavern, desperately seeking any sign of life. From every shadowed crevice came a deep, labored breathing, a sound that mingled with the dank, pungent haze seeping into the cave. The very walls exhaled this rank, decaying odor and it felt as though something watched him with unseen eyes, poised to pounce at the slightest display of weakness.

A potent, urgent command rang in his fading consciousness: *Stand up and get out, Mendal!* He tried, but a surge of unspeakable pain seized his body, twisting him into a fetal position as if tiny, ravenous vermin were gnawing from within his gut. Cramping and convulsing uncontrollably, he could do nothing to defy the relentless torment.

Nearby, hot steam spiraled upward from a small creek, offering a brief respite from his suffering. Seizing the momentary lull in agony, Mendal crawled toward the creek, only to have its edge crumble away beneath his weight. A surge of thick, gooey fluid erupted, engulfing him, dragging him beneath its murky surface. Panic clutched his heart as he struggled desperately for breath, clawing upward with every ounce of strength until, finally, he broke free from the oily grip.

Collapsing in exhausted misery, he wiped crimson streaks from his face, his vision still swimming. He crawled a few more staggered feet before halting, lost and bewildered, with no inkling of the path ahead.

A blinding beam of light cut through the gloom from one of the cavern tunnels, igniting a glimmer of hope deep within him. *I see a light! Coming to rescue me. A presence in the brightness. A presence of—*

It struck him! Fists of hardened leather embedded with spikes rained down, ripping through his face with savage precision. The unholy assault was accompanied by ear-splitting screeches and howls, etching into his faltering consciousness the grim message of his imminent obliteration, the embodiment of pure, unrelenting malice: the Rage of Lucifer!

"Mendal, this will not be fast. It will be long and excruciatingly painful. As agonizing as I can make it," snarled Rage in a deep, guttural rasp that resonated like the rumble of infernal thunder. "The more drawn-out your torment, the better, as there is nothing I'd relish more than to ensure that you cease to exist. I can prolong your suffering for eternity!"

As he spoke, Rage's form contorted into an unspeakable horror; his fingertips transformed into vicious blades and his eyes sharpened like deadly swords. With brutal precision, he stabbed and slashed at Mendal, the searing pain of every cut a testament to his diabolical intent.

Amidst sinister, mocking laughter, Rage unleashed torrents of burning acid into Mendal's freshly inflicted wounds. The acrid liquid seared his flesh until it shriveled and peeled away. In a grotesque act, he tore Mendal limb from limb, only to piece him back together, ensuring his torment would persist indefinitely.

This nightmarish cycle of agony stretched on for what felt like excruciating minutes that bled into horrid hours. Finally, lulled by a perverse boredom with the endless torture, the Rage of Lucifer began to speak through a voice that dripped contempt and cruelty: "It's a dog-eat-dog world, Mendal. Man is destined to fight solely for his own survival. The strong thrive in luxury, while the weak are condemned to suffer and die alone. Life after life, over and over, the strong will always triumph; the weak, forever perish."

"I am the one who is supposed to be God," Lucifer raged. "Your Michael has no real power and the Father in Paradise is just a silly dream of His. If God exists, has power and loves you as you say, then where is He? Why doesn't your God rescue you?"

The Rage of Lucifer raised his massive arms, with fists clenched, high above his head. "Earth is mine! Your death means no decision! So, no one can stop me from creating Radania in any way I desire!

'Majorities rule' makes me the victor, because the majority did not decide against me."

With brutal force, he seized Mendal's tattered, mutilated body and squeezed the very essence of life from it. Blood gushed from the gashes that marred Mendal's flesh and his brain matter exploded in a chaotic cloud of despair.

The Rage of Lucifer discarded him. No sooner had he been abandoned than the hideous, ravenous hounds of hell surged forth from the cavern walls. They swarmed over him with relentless fury. Driven by an insatiable hunger, they tore away every morsel of flesh that clung to his bones.

And yet, even as the semblance of life was stripped from him, a faint, insistent whisper stirred in the dark recesses of Mendal's soul, *You must try to save yourself, no matter how impossible it appears.*

Who are you? he managed to project from his fading consciousness. *My body is dead, how can I save myself when there is nothing left of me to rescue?*

A gentle, spectral voice replied, *You are a small flicker of blue light, hovering above your lifeless form. You must flee now, before Lucifer finds you.* For an agonizing moment, his delicate blue glow wavered perilously, poised to extinguish. But then, as if nurtured by the divine breath of God, it flickered with renewed life.

From within its light, Mendal gazed down upon his ravaged corpse. *There is nothing left to save. I cannot move, no feeling or hope remains.*

Urgently, the inner voice pleaded, *Flee! Lucifer will track you down, you must fight for your escape!*

At the brink of surrender, when all hope seemed lost, a ghostly figure emerged, a being of pure white light edged in soothing violet. The figure glided silently to Mendal, instantly enveloping his feeble blue spark with healing violet radiance that pulsed with the promise of renewal. *I found you when you were but a fragile glimmer,* projected the serene figure, *yet I cannot elevate you without your own will to fight.*

With a surge of vital strength, Mendal lifted his eyes in recognition. "Zee!" he gasped.

As Zee grasped him with an embrace of luminous warmth, he urged, *Please do not look back, Mendal.*

Too late. The ghastly sight of Lucifer's monstrous hounds feasting upon the remnants of his shattered body, even gnawing on broken bones, proved too overwhelming for Mendal's fragile spirit. A tortured cry escaped him, inadvertently drawing unwanted attention to their precarious flight.

In that moment, Mendal's blue light, now morphing into a shadowy form, convulsed with agony. A black streak shot from Lucifer had entered Mendal's psyche. "You think you can escape me, but you can't. Ever!" Lucifer screeched, his voice echoing with eternal malice. "I have embedded a piece of my essence into your soul. You will never be free, for a piece of me now resides within you."

Gently, Zee lifted Mendal into a narrow passageway where movement, although still strenuous, felt marginally easier. As they maneuvered through a perpetual maze of twisting tunnels weaving within the planet, Zee had to rouse Mendal from the brink of unconsciousness time and again. Bathed in the restorative power of violet light, Mendal gradually began to reclaim the self he once was.

Navigating a particularly tight corner of the cavern, Zee suddenly detected a faint, desperate cry for help. Pausing, he listened intently, straining to discern its origin. In that heart-stopping moment, Mendal's head jerked upright. "Lisa!" he cried out, his voice trembling with astonishment and long-lost hope.

Focusing all their attention on the sorrowful sobs drifting through the dank corridors, Zee and Mendal quickly located the source. Tucked away in a narrow crevice high on a crumbling cavern wall lay Lisa, hunched in a fetal position, her entire body quivering with fear and vulnerability.

Reaching out with gentle urgency, Zee projected his voice directly into her mind, *Lisa, can you hear me?* A slight twitch confirmed her recognition. *I am a friend. I can help you get out of this forsaken place and return you home.*

For a moment, she stirred and lifted her head, but when her tear-filled eyes met the abhorrent specter of the cavern walls marred by the pungent stench of decay, the glaring stains of dried blood and the repulsive traces of human filth, overwhelming terror forced her back into a protective curl. A strangled moan escaped her lips as she sank once more into her fetal posture.

Then, a bone-chilling roar erupted from a cavern below, jolting both Zee and Mendal into a sobering realization: another of Lucifer's nightmarish creatures was in relentless pursuit!

Acting without hesitation, Mendal scooped up Lisa and bolted through the pathway. The monstrous screeching grew ever louder and more menacing. In frenzied desperation, Zee and Mendal raced down winding side tunnels, each turn amplifying the jarring symphony of terror.

All around them, the anguished screams of tormented souls trapped in the cavern walls echoed as they clawed and grasped in futile agony. Panic surged as Mendal realized they were hopelessly lost, while the beast drew ever closer.

Summoning the full measure of his recovered strength, Mendal re-emerged into his true form and positioned himself as an unyielding shield before Lisa and Zee. At the final bend, the predator rounded the corner, its eyes fixated on its prey as it pounced with savage precision. At that crucial moment, Mendal let out a deafening roar, a defiant bloodcurdling scream echoing through the oppressive darkness, then—

Chapter 33

"John, what's wrong? Are you okay?" Leslie shook him roughly as she knelt beside him. John stared blankly with eyes as wide as saucers, his entire body trembled under the weight of numbed horror. "John, something really bizarre just happened. You screamed and for a split second, it was like a hideous monster leapt out of you," she continued frantically, scanning the surrounding darkness for any sign of the creature lurking in the shadows.

Slowly, John sat upright, his gaze distant and haunted. Matt, one of Leslie's hippie friends from school who had witnessed the entire unsettling episode, stepped over and joined their whispered conversation. In a hushed tone, Leslie confided, "Matt, John took some pure LSD," her words barely audible as she and Matt edged away from him.

"How long ago?" Matt inquired, his tone laced with concern.

Leslie glanced down at her watch, "It's been about two hours."

"He's caught in a bad acid trip, Les," Matt added. "I've guided many friends through these experiences, but I've never seen such a vivid apparition literally leap out of someone's body."

Overwhelmed, Leslie's eyes filled with tears as she thought, *What can we do? I feel so guilty . . . I gave him that terrible drug. What if this changes him forever?*

Deep within her troubled psyche, a dark whisper echoed, *Don't worry yourself, Fay; you did just fine,* the insidious voice of Caligastia projected from the depths of her mind.

"Nothing we can do now. He must get through this alone," Matt finally asserted. "We'll stay close until he comes down, an hour, maybe two at most."

Leslie and Matt carefully eased John onto a small mound of dirt tucked behind a solitary tree, an isolated haven away from prying eyes. She softly whispered, "Are you comfortable, John?" As John nodded in a slow, trance-like manner, the chaotic visions of his altered state seemed to fade. Then—

∗∗∗

"Mendal, you're back!" shrieked Zee in astonished relief.

"What . . . what happened, Zee?" Mendal asked, shaking his head in a feeble attempt to clear the fog that clouded his thoughts.

"You and the monster vanished the moment it struck us," Zee explained in a hushed tone.

"Lisa?" Mendal's voice trembled as he scanned the shadowed passage. "Where's Lisa?"

"She's unconscious, Mendal. It appears she's endured a nightmare beyond measure," Zee replied softly.

Mendal rushed to her side, gently lifting her fragile form into his arms. She let out a faint cry. "They're gone, Lisa," her eyes fluttering open to reveal a weak, fleeting smile before darkness reclaimed her.

Without delay, Zee enveloped Lisa in the healing radiance of his violet light and together they resumed their perilous journey, racing toward the surface of this cursed planet. Without Zee's guiding power, the journey would have been futile for many spirits spend eternity traveling Lucifer's caverns, in a desperate search for a way out.

Mendal's face, arms and body bore jagged marks of his infernal encounter; burned, discolored flesh a haunting reminder of his ordeal. Though time might heal the physical wounds, he knew his psyche would be scarred forever.

In the quiet aftermath, Mendal and the swiftly healing Lisa embraced tightly. "How did you get inside Lucifer's planet?" he asked, gently easing away to seek answers.

Clinging to him with desperate vulnerability, she said softly, "I went there for . . . for a conference. But he took me. He abused and tortured me, using me in unspeakable ways. He swore that I was his forever, but once he was finished, he discarded me like trash." Tears streamed down her face as she added, "I wandered those endless, suffocating caverns and all I could think of was you. I'm so sorry."

"You have nothing to be sorry for, Lisa," Mendal whispered tenderly.

Zee, struggling to maintain focus in the oppressive realm, placed a reassuring hand on Mendal's shoulder. "I can take only Lisa with me. You must remain here . . . I'm losing focus, we must leave." Gently, he lifted Lisa into his arms; still, she clung desperately to Mendal as if anchoring herself to hope.

"How, my friend, did you ever find me?" Mendal asked Zee, his eyes brimming with tearful gratitude.

"I was journeying through the frequency energy circuits," Zee revealed, "trying to forge a link with Michael when I chanced upon Lucifer's vile frequency. Realizing the danger he posed to you, I entered."

Mendal sighed, his voice tinged with resignation. "I sense that a part of me is still trapped in this damned place, caught in Lucifer's clutches, while a piece of him resides within me. I worry I'll never truly be free as long as he lives."

In a moment of profound intimacy, Mendal pressed a passionate kiss on Lisa's lips. "I love you, Lisa," he whispered. "I will always be yours."

In response, she choked out, "I love you, Mendal. I'll wait for you forever." And then, Zee and Lisa vanished.

As Mendal emerged onto the surface, he scanned the sun-scorched landscape and, although he knew it wasn't possible, it looked like a completely different planet. Amid the windswept sagebrush and gnarled remnants of long-dead trees, a town loomed in the distance.

Ghostly figures were engaged in what appeared to be a gunfight on the town's main street. The air was tense with the echoes of a bygone era. One gunfighter, his outline flickering like a candle flame, stepped toward his adversary, drew his weapon and in the fleeting instant before he could fire, was shot in the back by another who materialized directly behind him.

As Mendal drew nearer, the decaying, dilapidated town flickered in and out of existence like an old film reel. The western cowboy facade, with its saloons and weather-beaten signposts, dissolved under the relentless, blistering heat of the planet's twin suns. The structures slowly evaporated, their forms melting away like wax. Mendal muttered under his breath, the words barely audible. "Ghost town?"

***

Suddenly, John realized he was resting against a small mound of dirt behind a tree. The kegger was winding down. He looked at his watch and whispered to Leslie lying next to him. "It's been four hours since I took that stuff. I don't remember anything, but I know God wasn't there. Never again!"

CHAPTER 34

John's Ford rumbled down Interstate 90, barely able to sustain the 55 mile-per-hour speed limit. He adjusted the wide brimmed leather hat he was wearing and leaned back into the oversized seat of the '50 coupe. "I can't believe we made it over the Bozeman pass," John muttered.

"Me neither," said the two passengers in unison. Leslie sat in the front. Her friend Dawn, with light brown hair, sky blue eyes and a freckled doll face, sat in the back, her long knock-kneed legs stretched out across the seat.

"Next obstacle is the butt hole of Montana," John said with a guarded smile. "Butte pass could be a nightmare for old Betsy here. Luckily there's no traffic on the roads tonight." He affectionately patted her dashboard. "You can do it, babe."

"I really appreciate you taking Dawn and I to Missoula with you, John," Les said with true feeling, gently squeezing his thigh through faded denim. She scooted closer.

"This old clunker is scary enough to ride in without you distracting our driver, Les," Dawn said with a giggle. "I didn't know cars this old were still allowed on the highway." She leaned her head back against the overstuffed seat cushion and closed her eyes. Leslie chuckled and moved over to her side of the front seat.

John felt good today. More and more, though, that was unusual, definitely not his normal state. Ever since the acid trip a few months back, he found himself gripped by gut-wrenching anxiety. He remembered virtually nothing about the experience but couldn't help but feel as though it had something to do with these weird feelings of impending doom.

"Can you believe we're going to see Heart tomorrow," Leslie whispered twenty minutes later, obviously not wanting to disturb Dawn's catnap.

"Yeah, and The Mission Mountain Wood Band. I can't wait." John really enjoyed these excursions to Missoula. Deep down, he wished he had gone to college up there like most of his friends had. He got good enough grades in high school, but four more years of school? It just wasn't worth the effort. At least it wasn't after he started drinking. But that was something he didn't like to think about.

"I heard they're guaranteeing two hundred kegs of beer this year," Les said. She leaned back and closed her eyes.

John nodded. *Drinking's all we think about anymore,* he thought to himself. The blinking "star" he was watching suddenly split into two parts, one half traveling northward, then curving back in a northwesterly direction, the other half continuing its journey eastward.

What the hell is that? John thought, as he vigilantly watching the "stars" make their way across the sky. The easterly traveling object at times almost decelerated to a stop, then sped up. Its companion vanished.

The object continued its stop and go journey while John pulled off to the side of the highway. He knew this wasn't an airplane or satellite.

It's a UFO! Shit, he thought frantically, *I've got to get out and look at that!*

"Why are we stopping," Les asked through a yawn. "Do you gotta take a piss or something?" Dawn stretched and sat up.

John kept his eyes on the object as Betsy gently rolled to a stop. "Look through the windshield, to the right above the hill. What do you see, Les?"

Les gasped. "Is that what I think it is?"

John said nothing; words were not needed. They both knew what it was. The object pulsated in the sky, then grew brighter. Suddenly, it was gone.

"What's that above the highway?" John asked incredulously. A triangular formation of red, blue and green alternately flashing lights, approximately thirty feet from the ground, were slowly maneuvering their way down the highway and headed directly towards Betsy.

John, his eyes transfixed on the glowing object, opened the car door. Dawn let out a strangled cry, "No, John, please don't," her voice raw with terror.

"You're not getting out, John!" Les screamed.

Leslie tried to grab his arm, but it was too late. He was out and the car door slammed shut. John immediately bolted to the front of the car. *Don't leave! Don't leave!* He projected his thoughts as hard as he could. *Beam me up, Scotty!* The next instant—

***

"Welcome." The voice was calm, masculine and, oddly enough, even familiar to John. He could also feel the presence of two females and their energy was very strong.

It took him a few moments to organize his thoughts. A face came into focus for an instant, then disappeared. John instinctively knew he was in the UFO, but he was not afraid. His body felt peculiar, peculiar in a very good way.

"The sensations your body is experiencing, John, are those of your natural state of being," the voice projected. "When humans leave Earth in death, they return to this state."

"What! Am I dead?" John could feel a smile.

"No, John, you are not dead. You will return shortly. We need to have a talk."

John couldn't believe how wonderful he felt. "Who are you?"

"In a very definitive way, I am you and you are me. I know this doesn't make sense to you, but it is true."

"Are you God? We're the same because you are God and God is in everyone?" Again, John could feel the smile.

"No, I am not God." John could feel the being's power expand around him. "You are in a situation that, as probabilities have unfolded, could not have been avoided. This leaves you in an unfortunate state, John, that will worsen for the next few years."

John attempted to talk, but he was unable to form thoughts into words. *Be silent,* Mendal projected to his earthly counterpart.

"Evil resides within you and it'll need to be extracted. Probabilities indicate that this will be successful, but the only future any being can see is a probable future. Nothing is for certain."

John understood. He didn't know how he understood, but he did.

"Know in your heart, John, that I am always with you in loving support. Know that no matter how bad your life becomes, it will only be temporary. This is something you must experience. Go back, John. You will not remember our talk or anything about this experience, but you will remember this: when the time comes, ask for my help. Together, we can extract the evil that resides within you."

***

The moment John reached the front of his car, the craft, with its brilliant, multicolored flashing lights, appeared directly above Betsy. Les and Dawn were paralyzed with fear. The blinding lights were everywhere!

Suddenly, the lights were gone and everything was calm. John opened the car door, got in and started the car. Les and Dawn looked at each other. "What happened out there, John?"

"What do you mean?"

Again, the two girls exchanged questioning glances. The drive to Missoula was very quiet.

CHAPTER 35

“Put down the beer and get over here, John. It’s your shot,” John’s burly, leather-necked pool partner bellowed with a scowl, his grimy fatigues bursting at the seams. “Just make the damn eight-ball shot. We got quarters waitin’.”

John threw two one-dollar bills on the bar, picked up his beer, took a deep breath and focused. His head was spinning. Two years after graduating high school and this is where he’d ended up, drinking in the town’s sleaziest tavern, one of the few he wasn’t banned from.

It took all his concentration not to bump into anyone or spill his beer on his way back to the pool game. He slammed down his glass, beer spilling on the already soaked table, eyeballed the easy bank shot and smashed the eight ball into the side pocket.

The sound grabbed the attention of the leather-clad bikers in the smoke-filled room, as he had intended. He howled "Born to be wild" with the song blaring from the jukebox.

"Shut the fuck up!" shouted half the bar patrons. The room was draped in biker paraphernalia and, as the central attraction, a replica of a Harley was hanging from the ceiling.

John strolled over to his barroom companion, gave him a "high five," and shouted to the barmaid, "Another pitcher of Bud on these guys."

"Yeah, another pitcher is just what you need," said Steve, walking up and giving John a sharp jab in the arm.

"Well, you finally got here," said John. "What took you so long?"

"Some of us have jobs," Steve said, shaking his head in disgust. "You had one of those once, remember?"

John ignored the ribbing and smiled defiantly, chin thrust forward. "Did you see me kick the shit out of these losers?" he said with booze induced belligerence.

"Watch it. We're in their bar," Steve warned. The remark turned the heads of three bearded, longhaired, leather-clad bikers sitting at a table a few feet away.

"Yeah? Well, I can take care of myself!" John slurred, posturing tall and tough.

Steve grabbed him by the arm. "Yeah, like you know how to fight," he laughed nervously, quickly edging him away from the pool table.

"You drunk motherfucker," growled one of the bikers under his breath. With bloodshot eyes blazing and fists convulsing in anger, he kicked away his chair as he rose.

"Another fight, Wyatt, and you're outta here for a month," the three-hundred-pound bouncer said bluntly, his two backups nodding in agreement.

After a few tense moments, the biker dropped back down and guzzled the remaining half-pitcher on the table. He belched and directed an intimidating scowl toward John. The table cracked up in delirious laughter.

Steve hustled John to the other side of the bar and shoved him into a chair at a small table in the corner. John ordered a pitcher of beer and two glasses.

John and Steve exchanged mindless chatter for another fifteen minutes, Steve keeping an eye open for trouble. John's life had been spiraling out of control for a long time now. Steve knew his friend was heading for something bad. "When are you ever going to grow up, man?" he said.

"Screw you, that's when," John snapped, slurring his words. Soon the pitcher was empty. Steve got up, grabbed John by the arm and headed for the exit.

Before leaving, John broke free and rushed back into the bar and bought a six-pack to go.

Steve climbed into the driver's side of John's car. "Whose car do you think you're getting into, big guy?" John laughed, pushing Steve aside.

"Don't drive tonight, John. You're too damn drunk!" Steve said. "I'll get you home."

"I'm never too drunk to drive!" John declared.

Steve thought about challenging him, but John could get pretty nasty when he had a load on. Besides, Steve wasn't feeling too much pain himself. "You get me killed, I'll never speak to you again," he quipped.

John fumbled with his keys and finally managed to find the ignition. He revved the engine and squealed the tires, spraying gravel over the semi-dirt parking lot as he careened into the street. The car bounced over the curb and then slammed back into the street hard, zigzagging as he floored it.

"Yeah, that's right," Steve said, almost closing his eyes. "Make sure the cops know a drunk's out tonight." He sighed, shaking his head. "You can be such an asshole, John."

Unperturbed, John just laughed but not with any mirth. "Takes one to know one, buddy."

"Wait a minute! Where the hell are you going?" Steve yelled, realizing they were in unfamiliar territory. "This isn't the way to your place!"

"I just want to drive for a while," John stammered. "I'm fine. Really, dude, I'm okay."

After a few minutes, John opened up to his best friend, "I can't do it anymore. I just want to be shitfaced all the time. It's like something inside is stopping me from believing in God . . . something or someone!" Unable to focus on the road, John slowed to a near stop.

"Someone?" said Steve. His concern was genuine and even though he was a bit tipsy himself, it showed in his voice. "Talk to me, man. I'm here for you, dude."

"I'm having these bad dreams every night. The devil's standing in front of me and laughing," John whimpered. "He just won't stop. I want to grab him and kill him, but I can't reach him. Finally, I get him around the neck, and I squeeze and squeeze until he's dead. Then I lift his head and look at his face and it's me! I killed myself!"

"Too much, dude!" Steve was intrigued by the story but terrified by his friend's erratic driving. Not only was he speeding, but he was weaving in out of his lane, repeatedly crossing the center yellow line. "Slow down, man, before you get us killed!"

Overcome by anger, John slammed on the gas, sending the tires into a high-pitched squeal as the car barreled through a stop sign. A lone porch light flickered on in the darkness of the night.

"Watch it, John!" Steve shouted, eyes wide in terror as his friend roared down the eerily quiet street.

John did slow down, but seemed lost in another world, completely unaware, as he drove without consciously realizing what was going on around him. He saw the speeding van with the corner of his eye, but nothing registered.

"The van!" shouted Steve.

I gotta green light. Damn if I'm goin' stop. Fuckin' drivers!

The van, going 60 mph in this residential neighborhood, ran the red light and slammed into John's car.

***

"He's not breathing!" the paramedic shouted to his partner. John's face was slashed from ear-to-ear, his front teeth missing. "Get his heart going. Now! We're losing him!"

Steve, broken bones protruding through his jeans, screamed when the paramedics lifted the stretcher. They whisked him into one of the two ambulances at the scene. His face and upper body were uninjured, but both his legs were a mangled mess of exposed muscle and bone.

Four emergency vehicles lit up the night with their flashing lights. John's car was mangled by the collision. The other car had swerved between two parked vehicles and ended up embedded a foot into the side of a house. Residents, awakened from their sleep, stood around pointing and staring at the chaos.

Two policemen handcuffed the uninjured driver of the van and jerked him up from the wet grass. "Jim, it's that hippie bastard from Chicago," the police officer yelled to his partner. "Look what you've done now, you dope smokin' son of a bitch!"

The cop dragged Dean to the squad car and brutally forced him into the back seat, his head cracking into unyielding metal. The ambulances left with a blast of sirens.

***

A doctor, dressed in surgical scrubs, entered the room. He looked at John's mangled face and shook his head. Tears rolled down the cheeks of a young aide. "I went to school with him," she sobbed. "He's the nicest guy."

"I've done all I can," said the doctor, holding the hand of the sobbing aide. "It's out of our hands now," he whispered to her.

The young aide softly stroked John's forehead, her face etched with sorrow. The steady beep of the life-support machine was the only sound that broke the eerie silence of the early morning . . . until the beep stopped.

John heard a calm, yet forceful, masculine voice. "Reach inside yourself and pull him out."

He opened his eyes as wide as he could but saw no one. The ceiling tiles were out of focus and the lights were dim. He felt peculiar, as if he were floating or drifting. He turned his head and found himself looking down at his own body. He sensed frantic activity in the room but could see nothing but his own body lying on the hospital bed. *What's happening to me? Please God, what's happening to me?*

"Reach inside yourself and pull him out," the voice repeated.

Be calm. I'm not dead. Do what the voice says. John reached his hand into his chest. He clutched at something buried deep inside him.

"Grab him and pull; pull hard. This is very important, John."

John grabbed hold of whatever was inside him and yanked. It wouldn't budge. It was firmly implanted and determined to stay.

"You've got him. Pull hard. This is important, John. Pull now!" John pulled with all his strength. Nothing happened.

Please, my friend from the sky, please help me! John asked instinctively. Suddenly, he felt a hundred times stronger. He pulled again.

With a loud pop, he ripped what looked like a skeleton out of his soul. The skeleton instantly transformed into a towering figure. The men glared at each other; their eyes filled with animosity. John was face to face with Lucifer!

"Your life as John is over," said the voice. "It's time to make your decision."

CHAPTER 36

Two suns, ablaze as one enormous inferno in the sky, ignited electrical flames that sizzled and hissed through the moisture-less air in lightning-like patterns. Mendal, standing alone, looked up into the shimmering atmosphere of the planet.

Where was he? The desolate surface consisted of only sandy dirt and rock, with occasional pieces of dying sagebrush and dead tree stumps littering the landscape. Every grain of sand that bit into his exposed skin and every taste of dust on his cracked lips spoke of an unyielding harshness.

He slowly turned and scanned the vacant street directly ahead of him. Wind-driven dirt devils swirled out of control. Broken shutters slammed against rotting window frames. Rusted hinges creaked. Ghost-like figures appeared, peering out of broken windows and doorless entryways, then vanished.

He felt a chill sweep through his body and up his spine. His soul filled with dread, lessened only by a tinge of hope that somehow all that had been so murky would soon become crystal clear.

Recognition flashed over his face as he recalled this decaying, frontier ghost town. He was back on Lucifer's planet! A rush of power and confidence surged through his body and soul; confidence brought forth from his struggle to survive on Earth, a planet dominated by the rebellion of Lucifer. He steeled his will for the confrontation that he was certain would be inevitable.

"Show yourself, Lucifer, if you have the courage!" Mendal shouted. "Your reign on Earth is over. You and your followers will never again deceive innocent people."

Eyes peered through windows. Shadowy figures lurked at every doorway, alleyway and rooftop. The murmur of a gathering crowd penetrated the thin, fiery air.

The suns made Mendal squint. Blood dripped from his cracked lips and the heat blistered his face. He pulled down his cowboy hat to block the merciless rays. He adjusted the holster he found himself wearing; the .45's seemed to fit as though they were made for him. He waited.

Wind whipped around his body, forming a spiral of swirling dust. He took the bandanna tied around his neck and lifted it to his face. The excruciating pain of pressure on heat blisters made him cringe. He fought to maintain consciousness, aware that this moment could define his fate and that he could not afford even the slightest falter.

Mendal glanced upward to the heavens. He knew he needed help to survive, and he prayed. He prayed to God. He prayed to Michael. He prayed to survive this hell he was in.

Mendal fully remembered his just-ended life as John. He remembered the years in Dalamatia, Fay, Lisa and—

Zee! This is Zee, Mendal. Remember what you saw the last time you were here! Watch your back!

Fifty feet away, a figure slowly materialized in a swirl of dirt and dust. Mendal felt a cold chill. He glanced up to the heavens, smiled at the spirits he knew were watching and prepared to make his decision.

"NO!" a voice suddenly thundered from behind him. A wave of paralyzing terror surged within, its icy grip infused with a hatred so intense it could belong to only one presence—Lucifer!

"Do you really think I'd let you destroy me?" Lucifer said. His every word fiendishly devised to mock, humiliate and terrorize. The grotesque power of evil filled the air as he spoke. "You want me, Mendal? Well, here I am." Lucifer's arms rose and engulfed Mendal in a surge of his power. "What do you think you can do to me, all alone and by yourself? Do you really think I'm that weak and vulnerable?"

The evil of Lucifer sucked Mendal back into the interior of the planet. He was flung onto the hard, red-rock cavern floor. Dark amber hues glowed from the rock walls; walls that radiated an excruciating heat and unbearable odor.

Cursing under his breath, Mendal staggered to his feet, only to recoil in abject horror—Lucifer was waiting for him!

"Welcome to my abode, Mendal. You're back," Lucifer said with demented amusement, "and this time I won't quit until I know you're dead!" Fear overtook Mendal, a fear that told him he must remain here for eternity, for Lucifer never loses a battle. His mind agonized in torment as he contemplated the endless future that awaited him.

"You underestimate me, Mendal!"

Suddenly, an overwhelmingly powerful spiritual essence, something indescribable in intensity, something stronger than Mendal ever imagined existed, something dominant, yet comforting in His presence, blanketed Lucifer's planet with the righteousness of His love. Mendal felt his fear evaporate in an instant, faster than the twinkling of an eye.

The Creator Son, Christ Michael of Nebadon, shattering the boundaries of time and reality as known in this universe, spoke:

"NO, LUCIFER, YOU UNDERESTIMATE ME!"

Suddenly, Mendal was back to where he had been before Lucifer's interruption. Again, just as the gunfighter became physical, Mendal glanced upward to the heavens, smiled at the ghostly spirit forms watching and made his decision.

Mendal drew and fired with his left hand. The bullet entered the prince's skull between the eyes and lodging in his brain. Caligastia staggered.

Zee's warning lodged in his subconscious, Mendal instinctively spun, dropped to his knees and shot with his right. Lucifer fired simultaneously.

Mendal's head, pushed by an intervening hand, jerked to the right. Lead skimmed his left ear. Mendal's bullet struck its mark and anchored deep in the System Sovereign's heart. Both Lucifer and Caligastia crumpled to the ground.

Cheers, coming from all directions and locations, broke the eerie silence. Mendal slowly stood and scanned the street. The cheers became a deafening roar.

Mendal raised his arms in a triumphant victory. He had defeated his enemies. With fists clenched high above his head, he mouthed, "Thank you."

***

Previously hidden in the planet's atmospheric inferno, a seraphic transport became visible. At that exact moment, Mendal found himself aboard the vessel. He looked around, expecting to see angelic transporters, the pilots of these heavenly craft. To his surprise, he saw no one.

"Mendal," whispered a voice from an adjoining room. *What?* he thought, smiling, *that sounds like . . .* Mendal stepped toward the portal, his heart hammering in anticipation.

Lisa met him as he entered the ship's bridge, her arms wide open. They embraced and gently kissed. For a moment he thought this was all an illusion, a fantasy formed by his mind. But he quickly came to understand that what was happening to him now was more real, more truly substantive, than anything he had ever experienced before.

"I said I'd wait for you," Lisa said, taking him by the hand and leading him to the craft's control center. "And look what I brought with me."

Mendal smiled and nodded. She really was one of a kind and never ceased to amaze him. "Nice, Lisa. Where'd you get it?"

"On loan from Gabriel. A small gift to help make up for what we've been through, Mendal. And Mei was kind enough to agree to come with me. She's been great at helping me through my physical and mental therapy."

Suddenly, the seraphic transport vanished. Destination: Earth, circa 1978. It was time to help a friend.

CHAPTER 37

A luxuriously decorated bedroom was the scene for a nightly ritual between two lovers. The sound of passion filled the air. Fay, using her body to frantically slam the man to orgasm, screamed as she, too, reached the peak of passion.

The front entry door was completely kicked off its hinges. A massive cyborg soldier walked down the hallway, entered the bedroom and turned to face his targets. Although he was carrying no weapon, invincibility came to mind as the only applicable description of this creature.

Fay shrieked in terror. She leaped from the bed and, realizing she couldn't escape, cowered in a corner of the room, her arms covering her exposed breasts.

The man just laid there, knowing and accepting what he had feared and dreaded for years. The glorious honor and esteem once bestowed upon this prince of Earth had degenerated into disgrace and humiliation.

"Caligastia, in the name of Christ Michael, I have been sent to deliver you to the Ancients of Days. The decision of the last personality has been made, and I am proud to be the one to inform you of the verdict."

Caligastia's naked body rose from the bed in shame. Being stripped of all pride and dignity somehow seemed an appropriate ending for the man who instigated the rape and pillaging of the souls of Earth.

"The Lucifer rebellion has failed to poison the minds of a majority of the personalities detained on Earth." This voice of justice, this voice of righteousness, this voice of God, was heard not only through the room, but through the entire universe as well.

"Lucifer's stipulation of 'majority rules' has now ended this outrage against the government of Michael of Nebadon. Loyalty to Michael and the reverent belief in the Universal Father in Paradise is the majority decision."

The soldier yanked Caligastia up from his kneeling position on the floor and encased him in an impenetrable force field. He looked upward, nodded a signal and they were beamed from Earth to the seraphic transport above.

CHAPTER 38

Several of Caligastia's remaining staff gathered around the sign posted on the front door of Caligastia's administrative headquarters. "Meeting at sunrise, outside headquarters. Everyone must attend. No exceptions," read staff associate Nod aloud to the others.

"Maybe this will explain Caligastia's sudden disappearance," said Berg, one of the Andonite assistants, with a disconcerted look.

Nod turned and faced the crowd, now twenty in number and growing larger by the minute. His lips pursed with suppressed fury. He opened his mouth to speak, then hesitated. All eyes were on him. "Mendal!" was all he could say. He stormed through the crowd, hands thrown up in disgusted resignation.

The crowd broke into small groups to discuss tomorrow's meeting. "Like we don't know what happened," staff associate Cyril said bitterly. "Obviously Mendal made his decision and it wasn't what we hoped for."

"I heard Michael intervened on Mendal's behalf," said staff associate Rena.

"That's not possible," said Cyril. "Michael has a policy of non-interference in matters concerning the local systems."

"He made an exception," said staff associate Smit, walking up to join the discussion. Smit was known for his intellect and logical reasoning. They all turned to listen. "Gabriel saw Lucifer and Satan interfere with Mendal's decision in twentieth-century Earth. In his mind, this was a clear violation of the guidelines, so he petitioned the Uversa courts."

Smit paused to let the others gather around. "The courts agreed and decided to allow Michael a single disruption in the time-reality of Nebadon. Because of Earth's quarantine, it could happen only on Lucifer's planet."

"Lucifer will argue in the courts to the end of his days that Michael violated the guidelines set by the Ancients of Days," said Cyril, "and I agree with him. He should be vindicated."

"But we all know that Lucifer broke the quarantine many times," argued Rena, "and interfered with Mendal's decision."

Smit nodded. "Because of those violations, the courts, after careful consideration, decided Michael could intervene, if He so desired. When Michael saw what Lucifer had planned for Mendal, He stepped in. He wanted to make sure Mendal was allowed to make his decision without any undue pressure."

"And, as we all know now, Mendal decided for Michael," said Berg, "essentially killing both Lucifer and Caligastia."

"Of course, not literally. Only symbolically. No one has the literal power to end a spiritual existence except the Ancients of Days," said Rena, shaking her head, "and then only after proper hearings."

A tall, lean, light-haired man cleared his throat to speak. The crowd quieted. "I have been sent to speak a few words of encouragement," said the man with a look of rapture. "It is not too late to join the ways of God. He will forgive all who sincerely repent the rebellion and the evil ways of Lucifer."

"I don't recognize you," said Smit, his eyes narrowed with suspicion. "What do you know about the rebellion?"

"The rebellion has ended," he said solemnly.

"What will become of Lucifer and Caligastia?" asked Rena and Cyril in unison.

"We believe that all rebels who will ever accept mercy have done so. We await the flashing broadcast that will deprive these traitors of personality existence. We anticipate the verdict of Uversa will be announced by the executionary broadcast that will effect the annihilation of these interned rebels.

"Then will you look for their places, but they shall not be found. 'And they who know you among the worlds will be astonished at you; you have been a terror, but never shall you be any more.' And thus shall all of these unworthy traitors 'become as though they had not been.' All await the Uversa decree."

CHAPTER 39

The members of the planetary staff who went into rebellion and worked wholeheartedly for the rebel Prince soon discovered that they were deprived of the sustenance of the life circuits. They awakened to the fact that they had been degraded to the status of mortal beings. They were indeed superhuman but, at the same time, material and mortal.

Very soon after Mendal's decision, the entire staff was engaged in energetic defense of the city against hordes of semi-savages. In an effort to increase their numbers, Hammone ordered immediate resort to sexual reproduction with the tribespeople, knowing full well that the original associates were doomed to suffer extinction by death, sooner or later.

The presence of Hammone and these extraordinary supermen and superwomen, stranded by rebellion and presently mating with the sons and daughters of Earth, easily gave origin to those traditional stories of the gods coming down to mate with mortals.

Mt. Olympus

And thus originated the thousand and one legends of a mythical nature but founded on the facts of the post rebellion days, which later found a place in the folk tales and traditions of the various peoples whose ancestors had participated in these contacts with Caligastia's staff and their descendants.

The previously impenetrable walls of Dalamatia were soon in shambles. Small fires burned throughout the city while primitive tribespeople rummaged around in the ruins of the first capital of Earth.

One hundred and sixty-two years after the rebellion, a tidal wave swept up over Dalamatia and the planetary headquarters sank beneath the waters of the sea and this land did not again emerge until almost every vestige of the noble culture of those splendid ages had been obliterated.

The followers of Van withdrew to the highlands west of India, where they were exempt from attacks by the confused races of the lowlands.

CHAPTER 40

The long, narrow peninsula, almost an island, projected from the eastern shores of the Mediterranean Sea. The neck to the mainland was only twenty-seven miles wide at its narrowest point. The climate was ideal, due to the encircling mountains and the fact that this area was virtually an island in an inland sea. The coastline landmass was significantly elevated.

The great river that watered the Garden, as they called it, came down from the higher lands of the peninsula and flowed east through the peninsular neck to the mainland.

Van and his followers arrived at the site chosen as the new world headquarters. The site was the most beautiful spot of its kind in the world. It was the one bright spot on Earth, for the world beyond was engulfed in darkness, ignorance and savagery.

Van took a break from the construction of dwellings when Amadon, his Andonite assistant, pulled him aside. "Van, something's been bothering me. I know you don't like to talk about the Lucifer rebellion, but I really need a few answers."

Van wiped the sweat off his brow and sat on a nearby stump. "Go ahead," said Van, "this one time. I don't want to be caught up in the past. The Tree of Life has arrived, and the Garden of Eden must be ready when Adam and Eve make their appearance."

"Are the rumors about Mendal true?" asked Amadon, using his shovel as a leaning post. "Did he really fight and defeat Lucifer?"

"Yes, he really did," Van nodded. "And his decision was never in doubt."

Amadon looked at Van, his eyes narrowed with suspicion. "Then why did he wait so long to announce it?"

Van stood and stretched. He tipped down his hat to block the rays of the sun. "Before Mendal was stationed on Earth as a member of

Caligastia's staff, he got the urge to take a glimpse at Earth's probable future. During a break, he viewed Earth's history on a quantum probability computer."

"Probable future?"

"Its future at that moment," Van explained. "The quantum probability computer forecasts the future based on events it projects should occur. It was against the rules, but he accessed it anyway."

"What did he see?" asked Amadon anxiously.

"Earth had no future," Van replied. "Lucifer destroyed it."

"What?"

"In Earth's probable future, Lucifer destroyed Earth when Mendal announced his decision to support Michael." Van walked a few feet to the water well. He took a drink and rinsed his face in the cool, clear liquid. "Because of the system circuit shutdown, Jerusem officials were unable to prevent Lucifer from taking revenge on the planet that caused his downfall."

"So, when Mendal saw Lucifer destroy Earth, he didn't know why," said Amadon, beginning to see the wisdom and courage in Mendal. "But when the rebellion was announced, Mendal knew Lucifer would destroy Earth for siding with Michael." Amadon rested on one knee next to Van. "In Earth's probable future, anyway."

"Yes, its probable future at that moment," Van nodded. "The only way Mendal could stop Earth's destruction was to change the probabilities, by making a life-altering decision."

"So, Mendal decided not to decide." Amadon smiled at Mendal's extraordinary act.

"Because Mendal had viewed Earth's probable future without permission," Van explained, sitting back down on the stump, "he had to live as though he hadn't. He could tell no one."

"I see." Amadon thought for a moment. "Knowledge of the future by the wrong person could have affected the probabilities and resulted in disastrous consequences," Amadon surmised. "And Mendal kept his secret."

"Yes," Van said, "and he delayed his decision as long as possible. Lucifer had to believe Mendal was truly undecided for the plan to work."

"But no decision would have meant a victory for Lucifer," said Amadon.

"No decision was not an option," Van replied. "Mendal knew the authorities would force the issue. He believed in God and he had faith in Michael. He knew that was enough to get through anything." Van smiled and got up off the stump. "Time to get back to work."

"Please, just one more question," Amadon pleaded. "When the rebellion failed, why weren't the system circuits restored to Radania and Earth? And what has happened to Caligastia, Satan and Lucifer?"

"The system circuits will not be reinstated so long as Lucifer lives," Van said. "We are waiting for the Uversa courts to hand down a decision in the matter of Gabriel vs. Lucifer. Lucifer was taken into custody by agents of the Uversa Ancients of Days and has since been a prisoner on a transition sphere of Jerusem. Satan is also detained on a Jerusem prison world."

"What about Caligastia?" asked Amadon.

"He is free to roam Earth until the expected annihilation verdict is issued," Van replied. "But he has absolutely no power to enter the minds of men, nor can he draw near to their souls to tempt or corrupt them unless they really desire to be cursed with his wicked presence.

"It is true: 'He who is born of God keeps himself, and the wicked one touches him not.'"

The End